For my father,
who instilled the game into my heart.

The
TURNSTILE

STEVE GODSOE

"Fenway Park is the essence of baseball."

—Tom Seaver

"Baseball is a game of inches."

—Branch Rickey

"We're the best team in baseball, but not by much."

—Sparky Anderson

"In baseball, you can't kill the clock. You've got to give the other man his chance."

—Earl Weaver

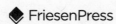 FriesenPress

Suite 300 - 990 Fort St
Victoria, BC, V8V 3K2
Canada

www.friesenpress.com

ISBN
978-1-5255-3605-2 (Hardcover)
978-1-5255-3606-9 (Paperback)
978-1-5255-3607-6 (eBook)

1. FICTION, SCIENCE FICTION, TIME TRAVEL

Distributed to the trade by The Ingram Book Company

Contents

A Genuine Sense of Wonder

I remember it as if it were . . . well, nearly forty-one years ago. But, for that opening remark to make even a lick of sense, I need to begin at the beginning.

My name is Landon Burgess, and I figure that, over the years, I've nudged my thighs through the revolving arms of Fenway Park's turnstiles over six hundred times. Yet even after all these visits, I still take in the games with a genuine sense of wonder, like I'm the eight-year-old version of myself and I'm seeing the Green Monster in person for the first time.

I'm not a season ticket holder and never have been. As far as seating goes, I choose to observe games from every vantage point the diamond at the heart of Boston has to offer. I've sat in every section at least five times, caught seven foul balls (two in the same game, go figure!), and even snagged a home run ball that came screaming like a missile off the bat of future Hall of Famer Jim Thome.

I was perched high in the nosebleeds during the '99 All-Star Game when a frail Ted Williams tossed the ceremonial first pitch. I sat close enough to kiss Pesky's Pole when Ortiz walked-off the Yankees in Game 4 of the '04 ALCS. And I had the privilege of sitting in the single red seat deep in the right-field stands when Jon Lester no-hit the Royals in '08. The memories of those games and a slew of others will live with me until the day I pass and am buried in my beloved Varitek jersey. But remarkably, those moments pale in comparison to the events of my most recent trip down to the ol' ballpark.

I swear to you on a barnful of bibles and the souls of everyone I've ever loved that the following is true. I experienced it the other night when I planned to attend an interleague clash between the Sox and the visiting Cincinnati Reds.

Let me tell you, I debated even leaving the comforts of my apartment that evening, as the sky had been teasing rain for the better part of the day. Despite the earthy smell in the air and the ominous clouds visible through my kitchen window, the undeniably sexy woman on the Weather Channel had pointed her perky headlights at a map of Beantown and said, in a delicious accent, that showers would hold off until after midnight. Come to think of it, the elements didn't actually matter to me at that point; she probably could've said a previously undetected hurricane was about to slam into New England with record force, and all I would've heard her speak of was sunshine and rainbows.

I have a circle of friends and family who I go to the games with, and I revel in each of these relationships. But I also enjoy spending the odd game with nothing but a single seat and the sound of my own thoughts running a private commentary. Maybe I just didn't want to drag anybody out under threatening skies, for not once did I consider anything but flying solo that night.

A good buddy of mine once told me never to trust a good-looking woman or a Boston weather report. So, with two strikes already against me, I played it safe and dressed for rain. I rolled up a waterproof poncho and tucked it into the kangaroo pocket of my hoodie, donned a vintage Sox cap, and hit the streets in a pair of North Face casual boots. The ballpark is a refreshing twenty-minute gait from my apartment, and by the time I reached the festive atmosphere of Yawkey Way, the sun had pierced the gloom with an ethereal presence.

If you aren't familiar with ticket-buying at Fenway, here's a brief rundown. If you wait till the day of the game, you're screwed! There's a better chance of being struck by lightning than coming away with tickets. Your chance of game-day tickets increases slightly if you go online, but you're gonna kiss a good half hour of your day goodbye staring at a screen that'll likely throw a SOLD OUT sign at you in the end.

And then there's the trusty scalper (yeah, the words *trusty* and *scalper* were just caught sleeping together). The general rule of thumb with street sellers is the closer to game time, the lower the price. A scalper who wants two hundred dollars at 4 p.m. will settle for forty dollars at 7 p.m.—mere minutes before the first pitch is set to fly. You've gotta exploit the window where scalpers would rather slither away with *something* in their pocket than crawl back into their dark hole with useless ticket stubs for fire kindling.

Sure, there are other angles and avenues for buying your way through the gates at Fenway, but considering the frequency of my visits, I've got a reliable connection for economical entry.

I made a line for a scalper buddy named Carlos. Carlos and I have been taking care of each other for years. All I have to do is give him reasonable notice that I'll be coming down to the game on any given day or night, and he'll hook me up with whatever tickets I need for marginally less than face value. I return his favours in the chilly off-season by bringing him the heat. And by that I don't mean Aroldis Chapman heat—I mean I service both his furnace and his mother's furnace free of charge.

The other scalpers who prowl Fenway's perimeter on game days are like regulars at a local watering hole. I recognize all of them when I see them and, through my ties to Carlos, know most of them by name. They know better than to waste a "Need tickets?" on me as I pass, as it's understood that Carlos always has my sale.

That fateful evening, I meandered through the crowd along Yawkey and then down to the corner of Ipswich and Van Ness, where Carlos can usually be found doing his thing, his booming voice calling out to prospective buyers and sellers.

I didn't hear or see him at that point, but I wasn't too concerned, being focused on the frenzied youngsters in Red Sox apparel stampeding toward me as if I were a matador waving a muleta. I braced myself, but they flocked past to the bronze statues standing behind me like giants just outside Gate B. There was Yaz tipping his helmet to the crowd, as he famously did after his final at-bat; Teddy Ballgame placing his cap on the head of a young Jimmy Fund patient; and, of course, the Teammates statue, a foursome of Sox legends, each standing with a bat over a shoulder as they jawed before batting practice.

I took a moment to drink in their euphoria before moving on.

With plenty of time before the first pitch, I embarked on a perimeter lap of Fenway in search of Carlos. If I'd had my phone on me, I would have called him, but I've settled into a nice little routine of late where I leave it at home whenever I go to the ballpark. I feel more in tune with the game when I'm not tempted to pull the device from my pocket every ten minutes. I've learned to open my senses to the live experience—watch the man one row down and three seats over relishing the lost art of scorekeeping, scratching the result of every at-bat into his archival scorebook with red ink; hear the crack of the bat as an opposing player sends one high and deep to left, then almost like a delayed echo, the ball clanking against the metal facing of the Green Monster among a chorus of oohs and aahs. On certain nights, I can smell the sea, as an eastern breeze carries the briny scent through the late innings.

As I moved around the perimeter, the weather turning dicey under a darkening sky, my quest to find Carlos, who is as reliable as the weather is not, was seemingly leading to a fruitless end. And I began to entertain a thought . . . perhaps a higher power was trying to tell me that my butt belonged on the couch that night after all.

The Ticket and the Turnstile

Shortly after circling onto Lansdowne Street, I spotted an unfamiliar scalper furtively making a sale next to a hot dog vendor near Gate C. A lanky man in a 1970s-era Pete Rose jersey with a messy crew cut and a pronounced scar from the corner of his mouth to just below his left eye slipped the scalper some folded bills and waited anxiously. The scalper flipped through the wad faster than a banker, handed the Reds fan his ticket without making eye contact, and was on the move before the buyer could oblige him. Then the scalper strode down Lansdowne toward Brookline Avenue like he had somewhere else to be.

I hustled after him, tracking him down near the ticket windows. Before I could speak, he was already asking, "Two tickets? A single?"

"I'm lookin' for Carlos," I said between breaths, brushing off his sales pitch.

The man measured me with dark, steely eyes and then slung an arm around my shoulder like he'd known me for years. "You the furnace guy?" he asked in an accent that showed he was far from home. A black beanie sat tight on his head, and grey stubble covered his skeletal face. He wore a faded *Dark Side of the Moon* T-shirt and green cargo pants.

I furrowed my brow, distrusting his forward approach and knowledge of my connection to Carlos, but nodded once in agreement.

He spoke again before I could find my words. "If you had business with Carlos, you now have business with me."

"You're creepin' on other people's turf, buddy," I said sternly, curling out from underneath his arm, and spotted a single ticket in the hand that had been resting on my shoulder, as if he'd pulled it out of my ear. He held it out in front of me and spoke buoyantly of the offering.

"Carlos says this one's on the house! Looks like he's got you high up along the left-field line. That'll getcha close enough to help blow it fair!"

I had no idea what the anonymous scalper was going on about, but when he finished, my instincts had me plucking the ticket from his hand.

"Burgess!" A raspy voice suddenly called my name from somewhere behind me. I spun and spotted through the moving crowd the familiar face of Johnny Scaggs, a scalper who's worked the Fenway fringe since the Buckner era. He was coming at me with purpose, weaving through the flow of fans headed toward Gate E.

"You seen Carlos?" Scaggs asked as he closed in, a query that was shaping up to be the question of the evening. A hint of panic defined his tone, and a weighty tension filled his eyes. I turned back to my mystery scalper, thinking he might be willing to loosen his tongue and start speaking some sense on the situation, but the only thing I saw was the building's aging brick façade. A sinister chill ran up my spine. The scalper had vanished.

Scaggs was practically on top of me. I slid the ticket into my front pocket without glancing at it. "I heard Carlos won't be around tonight," was all I could muster.

Scaggs shot me a funny look, shook his head as if it were *my* fault, and dropped an F-bomb that landed within earshot of a few youngsters. Before I could ask him if he'd noticed the scalper in the Floyd shirt, he was lost in the flow of fans like a merged vehicle. The sun had departed as well, retiring behind thick clouds of gunmetal grey.

I crossed the street to grab a quick cold one at the Cask 'n Flagon and was promptly drenched in the sweet aroma of sausage and onions from a roadside grill. A ten-minute wait to get in didn't deter my plan to bury a frothy mug of Sam Adams before the game, so I left my name and waited to be called.

I leaned against a Fenway-green lamppost directly in front of the bustling bar and slipped my hand into my pocket to withdraw the ball ticket for a quick study. It took me a moment to process what I was seeing. As expected, the ticket was in mint condition and boasted a Red Sox logo in the centre. But it was anything but modern. The colour was washed out, as if it had been left out in the sun for months, and the font was dated. The top of the ticket offered an entry gate letter followed by a numbered section, row, and seat. Below was a $12.50 admission price. And then, there was the kicker. In bold capitals over a faded red, white, and blue design were the words:

WORLD SERIES 1975
GAME 6
FENWAY PARK, BOSTON

The fine print confirmed that rain check information could be found on the back and the final line read:"Bowie K. Kuhn, Commissioner of Major League Baseball."

I flipped the ticket over and found a cryptic message had been jotted over the legal text in red marker:"RETURN BY THE 13TH."

I felt as if, at any second, I'd slip back into reality and the little reverie would turn to smoke. I was no longer leaning on the lamppost, and my pre-game thirst had been quenched with curiosity. Part of me wanted to show my newfound relic to everybody in sight, and part of me didn't want a single soul to lay eyes on it until I found some answers.

With a wary eye fixed on Gate E—the ticket's suggested ingress—I made my way back across Lansdowne, all the while struggling to recall my strange encounter with the scalper. It all seemed vague and patchy now, as if it had occurred in a distant past. I recalled him saying how my seat was situated high up along the left-field line, and how I'd be close enough to help blow it fair. In the moment, it had sounded like typical blather spewing from the lips of a salesman, but when I thought about the dramatic conclusion to Game 6 of the '75 Series, I couldn't help but shudder at the connection.

Sox fans lined the sidewalk in front of the gate, where a pair of green roll-up garage doors allowed access to four turnstiles. They were flowing into the friendly confines of Fenway at a good clip so, passing my ticket back and forth between my clammy hands, I joined the back of the progression.

I still wasn't sure what it was I was attempting to do at that point. I didn't have an actual ticket to the game, yet there I was, following some romantic lead à la Ray Kinsella. The ticket I *did* possess was a keepsake from what many baseball enthusiasts call the greatest game ever played. Entire books have been written on the improbable events that transpired at Fenway Park on the night of October 21, 1975.

I finally approached the gate and, like standard practice, passed through a metal detector upon entry. The turnstiles and their accompanying ushers sat abreast about twenty feet ahead, their tripod mechanisms rotating and locking with each passing fan as mechanical counters tallied the evening's attendance figure.

Of all the games I've attended at Fenway over the years, I can probably count on one hand how many times I've entered through Gate E. I figured that's why I never noticed an old, pedestal-type rotating turnstile sitting off to the side of the operational models. I didn't think it could be a Fenway original, but I guessed it dated as far back as the 1930s. It was a nice homage to the park's history nonetheless.

Its circular cast-iron base had multiple holes for anchoring and a tapered column supported four sets of tubular arms. The unforgiving hand of time had peeled patches of black paint from its surface like layers of skin, perhaps permitting ghosts of Fenway's past to leak into present-day proceedings. The waist-high relic was cordoned off with red ropes that sagged between stanchions and wouldn't have looked out of place if it were displayed in the lobby of the Baseball Hall of Fame.

I spotted a police officer the size of a Patriots linebacker posted along a wall beyond the turnstiles. He gauged the incoming crowd with a composed air. I envisioned myself handing an usher my '75 World Series ticket, and as much as they'd certainly be impressed with its condition and relevance to Red Sox history, they'd surely motion for the cop to address a possible entry infraction.

"Before the off-season, buddy!" shouted an irritable fan from behind me, goading me to keep the line moving and yanking me back into the moment. My heart started thumping like a kick drum, and my hands were so sweaty I could feel my ticket going limp. My eyes and mind were once again drawn to the antiquated turnstile in the short distance. Perhaps it was no more than a trick of the light, but it didn't appear to be quite as weathered and worn as it had moments before.

"Ticket?" An all-business usher before me eagerly waited to employ her scanner. She raised an eyebrow as if to ask, "First time at the ballpark?"

More reaction than action, I sidestepped the traditional ingress and made a break for the revolving relic. The usher stood stunned.

Just as a baserunner knows the moment his dash has been detected, I noticed the police officer bound into action to foil my leap of faith. I tossed a weighty stanchion to the ground, and like falling dominos, they all came crashing down in a clamorous ring. The cop was coming at me like a bull, his nostrils flaring. With my ticket clenched in one hand, I gripped one of the turnstile's arms and pushed. A mild shock buzzed along my arm and into my shoulder as I thrust forward. There was a slight resistance to the turnstile's pivot, but after a quarter turn, it seemed to work itself out. The creaking orchestra of old steel components tried to drown out the commotion around me but I still heard voices, though they were distant and hollow, as if spoken on the gossamer fringes of a dream.

Suddenly, I found myself in the middle of a timeless silence. An all-encompassing darkness accompanied the hush. I could smell sulphur and started choking when I seemingly popped out on the other side of the void. Vacant outlying voices leaked back into my surroundings, but they were no more than fragments of casual conversation. I was through the revolving access, and I braced for a mob of Fenway security.

The cop should've already been restraining me by that point, but he was curiously nowhere to be seen. And so was my revolving relic. In the turnstile's place was a slender man stationed behind a narrow booth of red and blue, his fashion sense sadly mired in the 1970s. He wore a flashy open-neck disco shirt and corduroy bell bottoms.

Two silver poles rose from the sides of the booth and supported a sign that read PROGRAMS $1.25. A voice suddenly boomed from the vendor, surprising me not only by its near-deafening strength but more so by the preposterous words themselves. "Programs! Getcher programs heeere!" He pronounced "here" as if he were carrying the word to the top of the Green Monster. I noticed two stacks of the glossy souvenirs before him. "Gaaame six, Red Sox fans! Getcher programs for game six of the Wooorld Series!"

Muddled in the moment, I looked to my ticket to confirm the match, but somehow it was no longer in my clammy grasp. I rifled through my pockets, but the search was to no avail. I didn't believe I'd dropped it because the ground in my vicinity was a Wrigley's gum wrapper shy of spotless.

I approached the booth, snatched a program from one of the stacks, and began to look it over. The outfielding trio of Yastrzemski, Lynn, and Evans graced the cover, and 1975 WORLD SERIES was printed along the bottom in a bright yellow font that nearly called for shades.

"That'll be one and a quarter, my good friend," the vendor remarked, his voice still full of life but, thankfully, down a few decibels from that of a bullhorn.

"You won't spin a profit at that rate," was all I could think to say. I returned the program to its place at the top of the pile.

Seeing as I was in the building and wasn't feeling the cold caress of steel handcuffs around my wrists, I decided to venture deeper into the mystery.

Smoke and Missing Pieces

Everything around me had a strange, ghostly air about it, as if it were retro night at the ballpark and I was the only one who hadn't received the memo. I marvelled at the thoroughfare of pedestrian traffic along the main concourse. People were really playing the part; there was an abundance of leisure suits, flared jeans and trousers, puffer vests, zip-up cardigans, leather jackets, and a sea of flat caps.

The attire was something else indeed, but there was more. To my absolute disbelief, I noticed a great number of people either had cigarettes, cigars, or pipes dangling from their lips, puffing away as if smoking laws had been abolished. A haze hovered over the moving mob, and the blended pungence of beer and smoke struck in sporadic pockets.

I maneuvered my way through the nostalgic parade and was impressed to find even the concession stands, prices and all, were on board with the evocative promotion. I hoped that, at just fifty-five cents a beer, there would be extra security that night, and then I realized they'd probably just tack on an extra zero to their prices when it came time for customers to pony up.

Suddenly, I began to feel cramped and woozy, like I was trapped in a smoky phone booth. I figured some open air would do me a world of good.

As I climbed a mountain of stairs that led out to the left-field bleachers, an admittedly pompous notion entered my mind that maybe the retro design had all been constructed for *me*—an elaborate tribute to my lasting allegiance, arranged by everyone in my Red Sox circle. It wouldn't have been impossible for them to rally a couple hundred volunteers, have them dress in a mishmash of 1970s garb, and make sure their cell phones didn't spoil the presentation. As grand as the thought was, it was fleeting. It turned to dust as the thought of the curious smoking entitlement clouded my mind.

When I reached the summit, the cool, fresh air feathered my face like a cure. With about forty minutes to go before game time, the stands were slowly filling with fans who, to my amazement, were also true to the 1970s theme. The grounds crew down below were set to wheel the batting cage off the field and put the finishing touches on the perfectly manicured playing surface.

As bemused as I was, I still managed to keep it together— that is, until I got my first glimpse of the Green Monster. What I saw of the iconic wall threw me a curveball that made Koufax's famous hook look like a dud: the seating section that had been added to the top of the wall before the 2003 season was *gone*, as if it had never existed. And the massive net that had once trapped home run balls that cleared the Monster was back. Seeing that just boggled the hell out of me, because I had actually purchased a square foot of the netting when they removed it and auctioned it off to Red Sox junkies like me.

At that point, my fears began heavily outweighing my wonderment. My heart started racing as if I were having a panic attack right there in the grandstand. I could barely breathe; beads of sweat dripped off my forehead and down my neck.

I grit my teeth and rubbed closed eyes with some force, hoping that when I opened them, the setting would show the changes of the last four decades. But when I did open them, all I could see was yet another major exclusion from the Fenway Park that I knew—the giant electronic scoreboard behind the centre-field bleachers (yes, the one with the John Hancock signature) was as nonexistent as a World Series winner in Boston for the better part of the twentieth century. I was certain there was no way they would temporarily remove a one-hundred-foot scoreboard for a retro-night promotion.

I know the idiosyncrasies of Fenway like I know my own apartment, and the more I looked around, the more I realized things weren't adding up.

The Coca-Cola Pavilion that should have been directly above me was an empty space that permitted me to catch sight of a muddy half-moon. Where the Budweiser Right Field Roof Deck should have been was nothing more than an overhanging shelter providing a bird's-eye view for a single television camera. I could go on about a dozen other missing pieces from modern-day Fenway, but the fact of the matter was this: it was quickly becoming more and more evident that I'd actually become unmoored in the sea of time.

I allowed myself to at least ponder that, if I'd indeed landed on the doormat of 1975, then a two-year-old version of myself would surely be defying sleep about three miles from the park in Lower Roxbury. As that rather eerie thought wormed its way into my fraying sanity, I was drawn back into the moment by the slow, gravelly cadence of long-time Fenway Park PA announcer Sherm Feller. That, of course, would be the same Sherm Feller who had suddenly passed of heart disease in

1994. What I hoped was a *recording* of his voice called the proceedings to order with his legendary opening line, "Ladies and gentlemen, boys and girls, welcome to Fenway Park."

As if Feller's eloquence was shepherding folk to their seats, the aisles around the ballpark began to host a descending flow of fandom. I saw activity in the Red Sox bullpen beyond the stunted right-field wall. From such a distance, I couldn't make out any of the players, but their uniforms were a polished white, and they were topped with cherry-red caps.

I swung around to the other side of the park by way of the main concourse. The entire way, I seemed to be pressing against the smoky flow of the crowd, upstream, as if defying the natural course of time. I scurried down an aisle that led me close enough to the bullpen to discern some faces. I told myself that if I happened to witness a certain Cuban-born ace warming up, I'd have no choice but to accept my place in the past.

My heart skipped into my throat when I first caught a glimpse of the pitcher's twisting, unorthodox delivery. After receiving the pitch, what could only have been a certain Hall of Fame catcher stood tall behind black-and-red gear and then flung the ball back with some zip on it. At that point, I was the only soul in the building who knew how his name would be forever linked to this game.

I nudged through to a railing that overlooked the Sox pen. There, right before my mystified eyes, was "El Tiante" himself, in the midst of another whirling dervish of a windup. Tiant's tufty sideburns and Fu Manchu moustache were unmistakable as he worked with a patented wad of chewing tobacco the size of the baseball he was firing at Fisk tucked inside his right cheek.

Though the phrase wouldn't be coined for another eleven years by *Boston Globe* feature writer Nathan Cobb, "Red Sox Nation" was all around me, and they were yearning to see their boys force a seventh and deciding game the following night. I almost felt obligated to brace those fans for a soft-hitting shortstop named Dent or assure them that someone who wouldn't be born for another month, nicknamed "Big Papi," would eventually heal the heartache induced by a play that started innocently enough as "a little roller up along first."

I spotted Gary Nolan getting loose in the Reds bullpen about 150 feet from where I stood. His fastballs snapped into the mitt of a player who many (including me) would call the greatest catcher of all time: Johnny Bench. I marvelled at a few of Tiant's looping breaking balls before Sherm Feller was back at the mic, asking everyone to rise from their seats and remove their caps for the national anthem.

It suddenly dawned on me that I didn't exactly *have* a seat. Shit, I didn't even have a ticket anymore, and when I did, I was too stupefied to take note of a specific section, let alone a row or seat number. I remembered only the words of the scalper I'd received it from: "Looks like he's got you high up along the left-field line. That'll getcha close enough to help blow it fair!"

As I glanced down into the bullpen again and saw a twenty-seven-year-old version of "Pudge" standing at attention with his hard cap held tightly to his chest protector, I conceded that wherever my seat was, it was far, far away from home.

Cruisin' Clarence

I returned to the nearby aisle and took in the swirling instrumental of John Kiley's Hammond organ. When the crowd roared in unison with the protracted final note, I began my ascent through the ovation to the shelter of the concourse. When the applause subsided, I heard Feller summon Duffy Lewis to the mound for the ceremonial first pitch. As the aging Sox legend hobbled out to the rubber, the roar returned as if it had only paused for a short breath.

While on the move, I spotted what looked like a janitorial nook next to a concession stand. It was free of pedestrian traffic, so I broke for it. Fans had become delirious in their push to have their asses seated for Tiant's first pitch, and at that point, I was a spellbound drifter who was only getting in their way.

I made it to the rectangular refuge, but not completely without incident. While attempting to veer away from the crowd, the cherry of someone's cigarette singed the back of my hand, and my spasmodic jerk nearly instigated a scuffle with a crotchety fellow who I figured to be long-dead where I came from.

A single black stool was tucked into a far corner of the recession, and though the symptoms of panic still lingered, it felt as if I'd relieved the weight of forty-one years when I finally sat.

I took a moment of repose to try to digest what had happened to me. Though I didn't know how it was possible, I'd come to accept that everything I was witnessing was no reproduction. I thought back to Carlos (or was that ahead?) and wondered if his uncharacteristic absence somehow tied into it all. I thought about the scalper who had so casually taken Carlos's place and how he'd pulled an admission slip to 1975 out of the ether. And I thought about the turnstile I'd never seen before and how it had played the role of portal into the past. I certainly wasn't in Kansas anymore, and I prayed the trip would offer a return ticket too.

A door in front of me slowly creaked open a foot. When it came to rest, an old, hunchbacked black man with a long-handled dustpan and tattered corn broom shuffled through at a speed that made Duffy Lewis look like vintage Rickey Henderson. By the look of his age, he could have worked at Fenway in 1912, when the doors first opened—less than a week after the Titanic sank. His hair was a smoky grey that puffed out from under a dark-blue visor, matching a knitted sweater he could have borrowed from Mister Rogers. He didn't notice me sitting there. I could hear him mumbling something over and over in a Jamaican accent, like a mantra, but I couldn't quite make it out. He headed out toward the bustling concourse, but then returned, sweeping nothing but dusty air into his catch pan.

The old man made his way in my general direction, still muttering his mantra like a broken record. Finally, he spotted me and paused, in both speech and motion, and looked straight into my soul with wraithlike eyes. Then he muttered again, this time with refined clarity. "Return by the thirteenth."

I was stunned to the point of speechlessness. When I found my tongue, it was too late. The feeble man had slipped back through the door by which he had come, pulling it snugly behind him.

I surged forward, but after checking the handle and finding it locked, headed around to the front of the concession. There I nudged my way into an open space along the counter and did a visual sweep of the congested workspace. I saw the door from the inside, but besides the dozen or so vendors running off their feet to stay on top of things, there was no sign of the Hunchback of Fenway Cove.

"Excuse me!" I threw my words into the flurry of activity. A snooty-looking woman behind the nearest cash register received them as if they'd slapped her across the face.

"There's a lineup, and yoh' ass belongs at the back of it," she said, drawing a long drag of cigarette and arrogantly blowing the smoke in my face as if to add an exclamation point to her directive. I coughed and nearly retched with the stench.

Realizing that what I *wanted* to say to the woman would surely have me evicted from the ballpark before Rose first crouched into the box, I remained calm and cordially asked, "I was just wondering if, by chance, you've seen the old man who keeps the floors nice 'n tidy 'round here?"

The woman scrunched up her face in a frown and took another haul from her smoky coffin nail, this time sparing me the reeky discharge. Maybe it was the subject of my enquiry, but when she replied, her tone had lowered a few notches on the crude meter. "If yer lookin' for Cruisin' Clarence, yer a little late. Swept 'is last kernel a few months back. Croaked right there in that little nook around the corner." She aimed her thumb at the space.

I figured that, if it was indeed Cruisin' Clarence I was after, she might want to know the ghost of his former self was still busy working unpaid overtime, but I left Miss Moody with a simple condolence instead.

While trying to casually drift away from the counter, I heard the woman call after me. "Hey, mister! What's your business with Clarence anyw—"

Without breaking stride, I let her words drown in the growing space between us.

I moved along the concourse toward home plate. Regardless of the inconceivable cards that continued to make up my hand, I vowed to watch Tiant hum that opening pitch in to Pete Rose. I was willing to bet it would be a called strike, and if his future was any indication, Rose would probably have loved to get in on the action as well.

The crowd erupted in a wave of approval as the Sox took the field. I still had a few minutes during Tiant's warmup tosses to find a spot along a railing before he let the first pitch fly.

Did I really just connect with the ghost of a former Fenway employee? I asked myself, still trying to wrap my head around the recent encounter. *Shit, I'm not even supposed to be here. How can two spirits removed from their own time intersect in another?*

The more I thought about it, the more I realized I was exploring an entire house of death. Though they were all alive and well in their contemporary 1975, where I came from, a good number of these people had long been ensconced in the earth. I swept that certifiable thought into a distant corner of my brain and then covered it with a rug and some weighty furniture.

An incorporeal version of Cruisin' Clarence had left me with the exact same cryptic message that was on the flip side of my World Series ticket, scribbled in red marker. I began repeating the directive words in my head, just as Clarence had mumbled his mantra as he swept the nook in which he had allegedly perished. *Return by the thirteenth . . . Return by the thirteenth . . . Return by the thirteenth.*

There was no doubt in my mind that the riddle was a warning of some sort. I had to assume that "Return" meant to go back to the time and place I had come from. "By the thirteenth" was still cloudy to me at that point. It was October 21st. If "the thirteenth" represented a date, then it obviously wouldn't come around again until November. I asked God to preserve my right mind if I was to be stuck in the past for another three weeks; I surely lacked the charisma of a Marty McFly. If the thirteenth was baseball related, then it could only mean an inning number, but it couldn't be specific to Game 6, as we all know how it ended dramatically in the twelfth.

The great Luis Tiant threw his last warmup and received the ball again after his infielders tossed it around. In a willfully ominous tone, Feller's voice resonated throughout the historic park. "Now batting for the Cincinnati Reds . . . Pete Rose, third base, Rose."

The name was met with a chorus of boos as an unfazed "Charlie Hustle" dug in and stared down the Cuban hurler.

I was up on the hazy concourse between first base and home, peering through the backs of heads and fedora hats as the first pitch landed right where it should have: square in the pocket of Carlton Fisk's mitt for a strike. I wasn't as close to the action as I would have liked, but given the fact I'd walked to the park in a different century, I couldn't exactly complain. Elation rose with the umpire's emphatic indicative gesture. It was a stark contrast to the absolute silence that would fall over the crowd in the top of the fifth, when Sox outfielder Fred Lynn would lie motionless at the base of the centre-field wall.

I lost myself in the wonderment of the first three innings before I slipped back into the inscrutable reality that my body was occupying impossible space and time. Just like the script, Boston was up 3–0 thanks to Lynn's first-inning blast to deep right, and Tiant was cruising right along, having only surrendered a single hit. I recalled how the fourth inning would be fairly uneventful, so while it played out, I planned to explore the rest of the concourse and maybe stir up some more ghosts while I was at it.

Zack from Blue Ash

The footway had thinned considerably since the start of the game, as fans were tied to their seats. I noticed another janitorial nook ahead on the left, similar to the one Clarence was haunting over on the first-base side. I was intrigued, but a little voice inside my head insisted I leave it alone and keep moving.

The crowd came to life with a Red Sox putout, and the sound rushed through the concourse in a sonorous flood. I couldn't wait to hear the place go bonkers when Bernie Carbo would surprise everybody in the park (including himself) with his game-tying blast in the eighth.

A food-and-drink concession on the third-base side had a pair of vendors standing before their tills, waiting patiently to serve somebody. I decided a forty-one-year-old cold one never hurt anybody, so I drew my shabbiest-looking single from my pocket and hoped it would pass the test of time. The dollar bought me a steinie of Miller Lite and a priceless smile from the young vendor when I told her to pocket my change.

"Still three nothin'?" the other vendor asked me with a tense look on his face that said it was killing him to be missing the action on the field. A sudden desire came over me to spill it all to the young man of maybe eighteen, to tell him how he should embrace the elation of the game's conclusion because a gut punch would come the following night when Rose and the rest of the Big Red Machine would roll to a win in Game 7. Not to mention the fact that nearly three more decades of titleless baseball in Beantown were waiting around the corner, disguised as an eternity.

"Still three nothin'," was all I offered, and I left it at that. I felt like I'd stolen something as I walked away with my cut-rate pilsner. The old-style bottle felt foreign in my grasp, but its contents went down in a familiar comfort.

I hadn't made it a hundred feet from the concession when I suddenly spotted a Cincinnati Reds jersey in motion up ahead. ROSE was embroidered on the back in red lettering overtop the number fourteen. No big deal, right? Where I come from, you practically don't belong at the ballpark if you're not sporting your favourite player's name and number across your back. But in 1975 Boston, a jersey that wasn't out on the playing field stuck out like a sore thumb.

The beer I'd purchased suddenly lost its appeal, and I tossed the practically full bottle into the trash. Trying not to draw too much attention to myself, I began moving as fast as I could without breaking into an all-out sprint.

Smoke still hovered along the concourse as if the ventilation system had quit with the end of the regular season. As I gained ground on my target I noticed his familiar lanky frame and messy crew cut. Though cautious of false hope, my spirit lifted. I thought, shit, maybe the scalper had sent a whole *handful* of us through the time-honoured turnstile and into the lap of the greatest game ever played.

How the hell do I initiate this conversation? I wondered as I geared down to a brisk walk. The crowd applauded once again, but I only heard it as a distraction. ROSE paused and then veered toward an opening that allowed him to view the field from our deep vantage.

I moved forward, stopping next to him and leaning against a red, heavily paint-chipped railing that was long gone in my Fenway. The steel was remarkably cold to the touch. As we gazed out over the sea of fans seated down the left-field line, our obstructed view (caused by the overhanging grandstand) still permitted us to see the lower two-thirds of the mighty Green Monster. Carl Yastrzemski was down in his familiar crouch with his back to the imposing wall. When Tiant came set on the mound, I turned to the man next to me, his facial scar like a meandering railroad track embedded in flesh.

"Lazy pop-up in foul territory to Cooper," I said with a calm confidence that implied I'd bet my life on the result. He chewed on my words while my prediction played out accordingly on the field. At that point, I still wasn't certain if he was my guy; he was playing his cards close to his chest.

"Well done, soothsayer," he finally replied after Cooper made the easy grab, the grin on his face telling me he knew he was no longer alone. "I raise you a three-run fifth for the Red Machine."

I matched the man's smile with my own. Neither of us knew exactly what we were experiencing, but we knew we were about to go through the rest of it together.

"I'm Zack, from Blue Ash, Ohio," he offered with an outstretched hand. "How'd you know I don't exactly . . . belong here?"

Zack was a long drink of water with sharp, angular curves at every joint. The colour of age was intruding on his brown beard, and his lower lip sagged next to the scar.

"I saw you make a deal with the same scalper I dealt with," I said, "the one who apparently offers passports into the past. And then when I spotted your jersey in the crowd, I made the connection."

Zack nodded. I had a line of questions locked and loaded when I noticed a look of desperation suddenly wash over his face.

"I gotta ask," he began apprehensively, "why haven't we gone mad by now?"

I'm certain he didn't intend it, but the soft-toned question hit me like a blindside punch. When I recovered, it was as if I could hear footfalls in my mind fleeing for the spillways, trying to outrun an answer that wouldn't quite suffice.

"I think it has something to do with the power of the game," I said finally, digging for something positive. "Baseball, yes, but I'm thinking more along the lines of this game, specifically. In my opinion, it's the single greatest baseball game ever played. And I'm willing to bet that even though your Reds wind up on the losing end, you still have to agree."

"Can't say there's a better one that comes to mind," Zack concurred. The distressing look in his eyes was already lifting.

"I think it's like a dream in the sense that we're somehow able to brush our fears aside and actually *enjoy* this," I added. "You can enjoy it as a Reds fan because you know your boys will win it all tomorrow night anyway. And I can enjoy it because the game itself is like the spine that binds the Red Sox history book. On the other hand, I think if we would've landed anywhere other than exactly where we are, we'd be singin' a different tune, probably in a room lined with padded walls."

Standing about three hundred feet from home plate, and about forty-one years from home, we continued to evaluate our circumstance. Through the Sox's half of the fourth and the drama that ensued during the following inning, we spoke but without missing a single pitch.

Just as we knew it would happen, the air was seemingly sucked right out of the building in the Reds' fifth. The game was all squared up at three, but the momentum had swung dramatically to the visitors' side, and we could have heard a pin drop. Zack and I knew that, for Red Sox fans, things were going to get a lot worse before they got better. We also knew there wouldn't be any more scoring for another inning and a half so we set off to roam through the fabric of a former time.

"So, how did you, you know . . . enter?" Zack asked hesitantly as we walked. His tone of voice suggested he felt he may be prying into something a little too personal.

"How did I enter the ballpark, or how did I enter nineteen seventy-five?" Rather than explain the particulars of my admittance, I decided to take him down to Gate E and show him precisely where an archaic turnstile had spun me into this predicament and then disappeared.

Once we landed at the bottom of the stairs, Zack told me how he'd received a '75 World Series ticket from the *Dark Side of the Moon* scalper and how Gate C was his designated access into the park. I was all ears as he began telling me about his time portal, which was in no way similar to mine, but then I noticed something that severed my attention from his words like a guillotine blade. Just inside the Gate E entrance, and exactly where I'd left it in 2016, was the old turnstile.

"This very mechanism was my portal," I told Zack as we approached the rotatable arms, forcing his account to the back burner. "A programs booth stood exactly in its place only a couple of hours ago, when I first washed up on the shores of '75."

Just as I moved in close enough to touch it, a stern voice diverted my attention. For a split second I figured it was my conscience speaking to me, but it was a woman's voice, though far from ladylike.

"There's no re-entry, fellas," a stocky woman wearing a humourless expression warned in a throaty voice as she approached us from out of nowhere. "Something magical just might play out on the field tonight, and you guys are down here flirtin' with the out door." A cigarette skipped up and down between her lips as she spoke, and smoke wafted around her face, forcing her to squint. A clipboard bulging with nearly an inch of paper was tucked under one arm, and FENWAY PARK SECURITY was stitched to the front of her navy-blue jacket in white lettering.

From the moment I first saw the woman, she rattled my bones with a bad vibe. I wanted to tell her we were doing no more than exploring the historical building, but I chose to put her familiarity with Fenway to good use instead.

"What's the story with this turnstile?" I asked.

Without giving the revolving gate so much as a glance, she took a mighty pull from her cigarette, shot us each a look of distrust, and then brazenly blew her exhaust in our direction. I was certainly getting tired of *that* act.

"Never seen it before," she replied. Her words were razor sharp as they cut through the smoke. Then she motioned us away with her clipboard, as if swatting pesky mosquitoes. We were disinclined to oblige her request, but we didn't need any trouble, so we took the high road.

We got about as far from her as a pitcher's mound is from home plate before she hollered after us, "I'll see you on the dark side of the moon!"

I halted abruptly as Zack carried on ahead of me. I recalled the scalper and his *Dark Side of the Moon* T-shirt, and thought about the classic album itself and its recurring theme of time and madness. I turned to face the security guard, and once again, the turnstile was gone. The security guard was leaning against the re-emerged programs booth, as if to laugh in the face of logic, while smoke billowed from her nostrils like inverted stacks.

Despite her trickery and clear connection to our other-worldly ordeal, I refused to let her break me. I turned my back to her once again and promptly made up the ground I'd lost to Zack. As we carried on through the spooky halls of the past, we kicked dirt on her memory until she was all but forgotten.

Carbo and the Shin Kicker

Before we knew it, the top of the eighth was unfolding before us like an old rerun. We'd ventured all the way out to the centre-field bleachers and were standing high along the back wall while the despondent crowd watched the Reds add to their lead. An inning earlier, George Foster's two-run double had put Cincinnati up 5–3, and Cesar Geronimo had just chased Tiant from the game with a solo shot to right.

"Whaddya do in Blue Ash, Zack?" I asked as Roger Moret was called in to put out the fire.

"Smoked meat specialist," he replied with a grin, all the while assessing the crowd down in front of us with a sharp eye. "Heavenly Smoke, downtown Cincy, actually. You heard of it?" I hadn't. "There's three in Ohio. It can be a monotonous gig—workin' long hours over the iron grill—but our joint makes a killing, and it pays the bills. Say, you up for havin' a little fun with our foreknowledge while the opportunity still presents itself?" he proposed, switching the subject as if it were a different station on a radio dial.

We were mindful of how the bottom of the inning would ensue, which was why Zack chose this specific place and time to toy with the past. We knew Bernie Carbo's pinch-hit heroics were about to shock Fenway into a pandemonium, so we planned to be camped directly under his game-tying, three-run blast. Zack's plan was never about necessarily *catching* the ball, but more about positioning ourselves close enough to be captured by NBC's cameras when it landed. We agreed that if and when we ever made it back to 2016, we'd find footage of the game, follow the flight of Carbo's deep drive to centre, and see if we'd survived the cutting room floor.

When the first two batters reached base in the home half of the eighth, the Fenway faithful stirred to life with newfound hope. But when Eastwick promptly retired Evans and Burleson, the anticipation of a big inning all but receded into nonexistence.

As the disquieted crowd watched a troubled Bernie Carbo step into the box, Zack and I were like volcanologists whose studies indicated that Fenway Park was about to erupt, and we knew it was time to make our move. Carbo, who later admitted to extensive drug use during his playing days, had been called on to pinch-hit for Moret and had no way of knowing that his defining moment as a professional ball player was only seven pitches away.

"I think row ten should be our target," Zack stated assuredly, and with no objections on my end, we began to make our way down the aisle. As we moved, we didn't have to watch the action on the field to know that Carbo was busy looking hopelessly overmatched at the plate. We heard fans all around us not only conceding the at-bat but also the game and, consequently, the series. Once we reached our vertical reference, we had about a minute to decide how far into the congested row we'd dare to venture.

Edgy fans understandably cursed our timing as we squeezed past them, and a particularly irate gentleman felt it necessary to boot me square in the shin. The man was built like a rugged lumberjack, towering over everyone in the row. His bushy beard indicated he probably hadn't touched a razor in over a year and, no word of a lie, his sausage fingers were curled around the necks of two steinies per hand.

The burly man must have used every inch he had to line up the vicious blow to my lower leg because it felt like he'd used a goddamn steel mallet to do the deed. As much as I didn't want that prick to see the sheer agony in my eyes, I'm certain he did and, pardon the pun, got a kick out of it as well.

"Outta the way, asshole!" he barked after landing his cheap shot. His breath rained down on me like a follow-up punch to the face, smelling like he'd been chewing on a cigar dipped in turpentine. Given our scheme, I had no choice but to swallow my pride and keep moving.

I followed Zack with a limp and a grimace for another dozen steps before he suddenly stopped mid-row, as if he'd reached an invisible wall.

"This feels about right."

People were spitting profanities at us like darts when a wave of deafening jubilation drowned out the anger. Carbo's improbable blast was on its way.

As the ball took its high, arcing trajectory toward us, the park became so loud that it rivalled silence. In that moment, time slowed to a crawl, and I envisioned the shin-kicker taking the three-run shot square in the teeth. As blood coursed down through his beard and found his plaid attire, thirty-five thousand frenzied fans cheered the perfect counterblow.

I pulled away from that fanciful sequence just in time. The ball was coming directly at us, and I thought I might be able to reach up and make a clean catch, but at the last second, it lost some steam and tailed to the left. The epic home run landed two rows in front of us and two seats over from where Zack "felt about right."

It was so loud I couldn't hear myself think, and I swear the entire building was shaking. I once read that the sound emanating from Fenway after Carbo's round-tripper could be heard up to two miles away, but after experiencing the fireworks firsthand, I wouldn't doubt that it actually travelled as far as three or four.

Even though we didn't end up with the ball, we were more than happy with the result of our positioning. We were high-fiving the very people who had cursed our mere presence only seconds prior as we celebrated the historic moment with a houseful of inferior fans who hadn't seen it coming.

Cecil Cooper had already struck out to end the frame before the crowd began to temper their elation. Heading into the ninth, the score was knotted at six, and we were on the move once again.

The Elevator

My shin throbbed as we shuffled through the rest of the row and gained the opposite aisle. A tunnel down to our right led us under the stands and back to the common artery that was the Fenway concourse. I could've counted on one hand how many people were in sight once we got there—it was crunch time during Game 6 of the frickin' World Series, and fans were either glued to their seats or standing nervously before them.

Like words spoken from beyond the grave, Sherm Feller's voice permeated the hollow concourse through speakers that were tucked into high corners and looked ancient even by 1975 standards. Before announcing Joe Morgan to the plate to lead-off the ninth, Feller delivered an audio bulletin that rattled me cold.

"Your attention please," he began. "For those of you who've been advised to return by the thirteenth, be sure to have all preparatory measures in good order."

Dumbstruck, I promptly studied Zack's reaction. His deadpan expression told me that the message had either flown unnoticed over his head like a commercial airliner, or he *had* heard the words, and they just didn't carry any weight with him.

"Please tell me you just heard that!" I seized his attention with a sudden blast of emotion, pointing to the high speakers. "Over the *fucking PA!* You had to've heard it!"

He shot me a confused look. "If you're referring to Morgan being announced, then yes, I heard it."

We quickly concluded that was all he'd heard. Once again, I felt like Ray Kinsella, except instead of hearing voices in the breezy cornfields of Iowa, I was hearing them in the smoky cracks of the past.

I decided to throw the riddle right out there for Zack like a batting-practice fastball, hoping he could knock it right out of the park. "If I were to tell you that, given your current situation, you had to return by the thirteenth, what would that mean to you?"

In a low murmur indicating deep thought, he slowly repeated the phrase two times and then asked, "Why?"

"It was jotted on the back of my ticket." I omitted the fact that a shuffling dead man had also dropped the phrase on me.

"Maybe this isn't exactly *our* past," he said with casual confidence, as if he were a university professor starting into a lecture. "Maybe this isn't the past that lines up with our present."

His theory sent my head for a spin, and I stopped him right there. "How the hell did you get that out of 'return by the thirteenth?' And besides—take the game, for instance—I'd say things seem to be lining up exactly as they should."

"So far," Professor Zack countered.

"So, let me get this straight," I continued. "You think aside from dealing with time travel we might've also jumped the tracks into a freakin' parallel world?"

"Not quite, but that moment could soon be upon us. This world could be on the verge of branching off in a different direction from the only world we know. Maybe this version of the game extends to at least a thirteenth inning and if we don't find a way to return before then, we'll be stuck here in an alternate 1975 or eventually return to a 2016 that won't resemble our own in any way, shape, or form."

Bewildered beyond explanation, yet impressed with his diverging-world supposition, I gauged the man from Blue Ash. All I could see was that damn scar and its chilling semblance to his theory—how it seemed destined for his eye but deviated just before the lower lid.

"I have to ask because I'm unclear," I uttered. "Did your ticket have a 'return by' number on the back?"

Zack shook his head solemnly. "Vanished somewhere down the line. Never even thought to look at the reverse side."

"Well, for shits and giggles, whaddya say we just assume the exact same thing *was* written on yours as well? Keeps us on the same page, ya know?"

"Sounds good," he said with some bounce. "Two against history, buddy."

As much as we wanted to go back out and watch the Sox squander their golden opportunity to win the game in the bottom of the ninth, we figured, if we were going to ride Zack's profound theory, we only had a little over an hour to find our way home. As we made our way to the scene of his arrival, Zack, his initial explanation of how he'd entered 1975 having been cut short, detailed the entirety of his downright chilling events.

"Just before the turnstiles at Gate C, I saw a green elevator off to my left. All I can say is that it just sort of . . . called to me. I don't know why—it was the same dingy-green colour as everything else in this place, and I wasn't even sure it was operational. I approached the lift with my ticket in hand, and the doors slowly slid open from the middle, as if they were the jaws of a motion-activated mouth. I progressed as if in a trance, and before I knew it, the rattletrap cab had swallowed me whole.

"Inside, the smell of sulphur was so strong I nearly choked on it. The display board offered a total of thirteen buttons, all in a single vertical row, and each button had a red number thirteen on its clear, circular face. I didn't dare touch a single one. Then the cab started to descend by itself. After a few seconds, I was in total darkness, and as the elevator picked up speed, the red thirteens began flashing like a crimson seizure. I must've blacked out because the next thing I remember is lying on the floor in a mental fog, the doors laboriously opening on solid ground. I dragged my ass off that hell ride faster than you can say Garciaparra!"

I shivered at his account. *At least I was spared the horror,* I told myself. And then it suddenly hit me like a revelation.

"That's it!" I blasted the words loud enough to turn the few heads in sight. "That's the fucking riddle—the elevator is the thirteenth!"

Just when we were certain we'd seen the last of her, we noticed the security guard who'd found us wandering down by the turnstile. She was stationed before the rickety ride that had lowered Zack into the past. As we approached the elevator, she gave us the same sombre look as before. A cigarette occupied her lips once again, and when she spoke through the rising smoke, her words were like a familiar recording. "There's no re-entry, fellas." It was as if she'd never seen us before. "Something magical just might play out on the field tonight, and you guys are down here flirtin' with the out door."

At that point, we were feeling the pinch of the clock and weren't about to let her stand between us and our outlet. We ran at her, trying to dodge past to get to the elevator button but she grabbed at us. She was tough as nails, I'll give her that. When she wasn't holding us off with her hefty arms, she was swinging her clipboard at our throats like a scythe.

As we struggled, I managed to hold her in check, yelling, "Run for it, Zack!" and he made for the elevator. The doors slid open without the touch of a button and he threw himself inside. I sprung from the guard and broke for the opening when the sweep of her leg sent my right knee crashing down onto the unforgiving concrete. My chin smashed the ground, and it felt as if I bit the tip of my tongue clean off. My eyes welled up from the impact, and through the blur I noticed Zack fighting a losing battle with the elevator doors. They were closing on him without his consent, and by the time I'd found my feet again, he was lost behind the steel curtain.

I hobbled to the lift on my abused legs and tried to force the doors open with everything I had, but the jaws were locked. I could hear the sound of grinding gears and squeaky pulleys stirring to life on the other side, and echoes of clanking movement filled the hollow shaft.

While Zack was climbing back into the twenty-first century, I was left to face the woman who was hell-bent on keeping me buried in the past.

Seeking Sherm

I turned and braced myself for violence, but all I saw was a backdrop of steel columns and deserted concession stands. A few people in the distance roamed aimlessly through the concourse as if the greatest game of all time was of no interest to them. After checking my periphery to rule out a broadside attack, I realized I was mysteriously, yet thankfully, in the clear.

I took a deep breath and tried to gather myself. My mouth tasted like liquid copper, and the pain in my knee was so bad it had me considering medical attention. Having already experienced the joys of a cigarette burn and an angry boot to the shin, I figured that if I ever found my way home, I'd be bringing back wounds like ballpark souvenirs.

I didn't need an inner voice to tell me that the elevator wasn't for me. I had no choice but to believe that "return by the thirteenth" meant something else. I recalled how Sherm Feller had taken to the loudspeaker before the start of the ninth and advised the lucky thirteens to have all preparatory measures in good order. Lacking the time and patience to work my way through the riddle, I decided to seek out the source and get to the bottom of things by heading straight to the top.

From where I'd last seen Zack and the dour security guard, I made the long swing around the concourse to the third-base side of home plate. This was where my familiarity with the ins and outs of Fenway Park finally began to play into my hand. Over the years, I've been on three press-box tours, and I prayed that the access that led upstairs would still be in the same place during the '70s.

With the Gate A entrance in sight, I could see a simple green door along the brick wall marked STAFF ONLY. I knew that on the other side was a corridor that would offer access to a stairwell and another elevator. If the past and present aligned, a spring-loaded door at the end of the passage should grant access to Yawkey Way.

Walking up to the STAFF ONLY door, I turned the sturdy handle but to no avail. I went to a nearby trash can and took out a seemingly untouched newspaper. With my back and the flat of my foot resting against the wall, I spent the next ten minutes or so standing directly next to the employee entrance, trying not to look too suspicious as I rolled the paper into a compact baton.

When the door finally clicked and swung open, I positioned the newspaper between the steel frame and the door, holding it in place while the door slowly crept back toward the closed position. The staff member who'd unknowingly granted me access into the corridor was in too much of a hurry to look back and make sure the latch had been secured. Lucky for me. With the door resting slightly ajar, I held onto the handle, discreetly removed the *Daily Wedge* and slid through.

The corridor had a cavernous feel, with sombre lighting and a musty odour that seemed to seep through the cracks in the mortar. The elevator was flagged with yellow safety tape, and a standing sign informed that the lift was down due to mechanical repair. I pictured an irritable Sherm Feller having to drag his butt up five flights of stairs on a nightly basis.

Where a door equipped with a keypad hangs in 2016 was no more than an open frame leading to another corridor of sorts. The lighting was so poor within the small space that I wondered how anybody ever got to where they were going. My vision struggled to discern that a door at the end of the space was propped open with a small stack of bricks, as if they'd been plucked from the walls, showing a set of stairs beyond leading up to the press box.

The sound of a voice drifted down the stairwell, and though I couldn't make out the muffled words, I knew Feller was announcing a Red to the plate in the top of the eleventh inning. The man with the celebrated voice was doing his thing almost directly above me, and from where I was positioned, it almost felt like I could've been an annoying tickle in the depths of his throat.

The cold concrete steps had definitely seen better days. It appeared as if notable defects were continuously being masked under layers of the park's customary green paint. The sections of wall that accompanied each landing were embellished with beautifully framed photos of Red Sox legends. A nice touch was added to the final flight of stairs, with signed baseball bats acting as spindles.

Slightly winded from the climb, I reached a final landing that led to a set of double doors. I supposed that security must have had all their trust invested in the single door on the concourse level because I casually pushed through the doors as if I were a member of the Fenway press.

The doors opened on what appeared to be a lounge area. The walls were a smoky yellow, and a trinity of tacky sofas occupied the space. A woman who looked to be a short-order cook was dozing with her feet up on a coffee table, a cigarette smouldering to its demise in her slackened fingers. I didn't need to know her to know that her day had been long—but not nearly as long as mine.

As lax as security was to that point, I still didn't take a single step for granted. I knew I was in a restricted area and that, if I ran into the wrong person, I would be escorted out of the building and likely turned over to the BPD.

Though no one else was in sight, I tried to look like I belonged as I ventured deeper into the lounge. Modern-day collectors of classic cigarette and soda vending machines would kill for the models lining the walls. Those walls ultimately wound into a smaller hallway that offered access to a cafeteria and the inoperative elevator.

I continued around a sharp corner and there it was, beyond yet another set of double doors wide open with the assistance of kick-down door stops: the long, sweeping corridor that ran behind the multiple booths overlooking the field. Even if I were blindfolded, I would have known where I was; I could hear the clatter of clicking typewriter keys as a slew of columnists feverishly spun their take on the events transpiring below.

I knew that Feller's booth was located directly behind home plate, so I pressed on. The first door was marked Booth A, and a square pane of glass allowed me to peek through and see the backs of about a dozen seated men. Their eyes were fixed on the tense action as they impulsively typed away through swirls of lazy smoke billowing skyward.

The game was so thrilling my passage went undetected. Nobody dared turn away from a single pitch for fear of missing a monumental moment. *Don't even blink, boys,* I mused as I stepped carefully past, *the big blast will soon be high up along the left-field line.*

As I approached Booth B, I saw the door propped wide open with a rubber wedge. This far inside, even a single glance aimed at the wrong person could prove costly, so I kept my head down and didn't break stride. The doors to booths C and D were side by side, and I knew that the man I was seeking would be doing his thing behind one of them. When I spotted an NBC logo shoddily taped to the door of the first booth, I knew Feller had to be camped in the other.

I took a deep breath and peered through the eye-level glass. The cramped booth was rustic and partially open-aired, like a duck blind. And there, seated behind a Plexiglas screen that protected his tools of the trade from the elements, was the lyrical legend himself, a fifty-seven-year-old version of Sherm Feller.

My first image of Feller was of him sitting before his public-address microphone wearing a cozy houndstooth overcoat and a grey fedora hat stylishly tilted and pivoting his torso as he spoke to a gentleman seated next to him. They shared a brief laugh, and then Feller rose to his feet and casually walked toward me. I froze like a deer in the headlights. My eyes were still glued to the glass opening when he opened the door.

"Well it's about bloody time, Burgess!"

The Yellow Button

Speaking as if he'd been expecting me, Feller's voice was grainy and gruff, like whatever he'd been smoking had been wrapped in sandpaper. The man exuded confidence, and his sprightly eyes called for me to explain my tardiness.

"How do you—"

"—know your name?" Feller finished. He turned to head back into the booth and beckoned me to follow. "You know *my* name," he said just before he settled back into his seat, "so why the hell shouldn't I know yours?"

I felt so damn unhinged by his physical presence; this was so much more than just hearing his voice over the PA. Time travel—been there, done that. Diverging worlds—to be determined. But I couldn't for the life of me understand how or why a 1975 model of Sherm Feller not only knew my name but was also speaking to me as if I were late for a meeting.

I stepped lightly across the threshold and into a narrow access that fed into the booth. The other person within the tight space was a gentleman of about forty, who I assumed to be Feller's assistant. Sherm asked him to vacate the booth, and once he'd complied, Feller offered me his place before the Plexiglas. Haphazardly arranged at the workstation were scribbled notes, newspapers, a pair of heavily used ashtrays, and the equipment required to send Feller's gravelly tone out over the masses like a warm blanket.

On the base of his PA microphone were three buttons, each the same shape as, but slightly smaller than, a domino. The first two were black and the third a creamy yellow.

Feller raised an index finger as if to say, "One second." Then, with the same finger, he pressed firmly on the yellow button and, while holding it in place, leaned in to the mic and confirmed where we stood within the game. "Leading off the bottom of the eleventh, Rick Miller, pinch-hitter, Miller."

To keep all of Fenway from what he knew would be our most uncanny of conversations, he released the button and turned to face me. After an awkward moment where he seemed to be auditing his own musings, he said, "You just missed Evans's spectacular catch in right to end the top of the inning. That one never gets old."

It took me a second to process that final five-word sentence. "You say that as if you've seen the play before." My words sounded distant and hollow, as if a forty-one-year divide existed between my lips and Feller's ears. The crowd was still buzzing after witnessing Evans's game-saving grab at the wall. He'd miraculously stolen a potential home run off the bat of Joe Morgan, regained his balance, and threw to first to double-up a speedy Griffey.

Feller chuckled to himself and then reunited his fingers with a cigar resting in the ashtray. "To say I've seen that play before would be an astronomical understatement."

He took a few puffs on his stogie and glanced out over the field, leisurely retrohaling the smoke into the crisp, ripening night. It was vintage Sherm Feller right before my eyes, and it was absolutely mind blowing!

"I've seen this particular game—or I should say *variations* of this particular game—more times than I could begin to count," Feller continued. "Up until the instant where Fisk makes contact in the bottom of the twelfth, the game always plays out like a script, right down to the finest detail. But from that moment on, worlds fan out into a countless number of distinct variations, and the game ends in a countless number of different ways. Pudge always manages to make some form of contact with that world-diverging pitch. I've seen everything from a violent comebacker that literally fractures Darcy's tibia, to my favourite one of all—the one you're lucky enough to know as one of the greatest moments in baseball history."

Pat Darcy retired Miller on a fly-out to left, and Feller's finger was ready on the yellow button to announce Doyle. I couldn't help but find myself thinking of Zack, and how the theory he'd seemingly plucked out of thin air had essentially been echoed by the legendary announcer.

"What happens in this at-bat with Doyle?" I asked, feeling like I was poking an uncaged bear.

"Routine grounder to short on the fourth pitch," he replied in a fashion that suggested he'd hoped to at least be challenged. "Yaz follows with a carbon-copy ground ball to end the frame."

If I were watching a live game in 2016 and someone sitting next to me was correctly predicting the outcome of every at-bat, I'd surely be dumbfounded and at a loss for words. But given the circumstances, I continued pressing Feller for more answers.

"Who comes out on the winning end of *this* particular game six?"

His face turned sour. "Like I said, all I ever know is what happens up until the Fisk at-bat in the twelfth. After that it's anyone's guess. But what I can—and *have*—told you is that you need to return by the thirteenth inning."

So there it was, finally, some verification as to what the hell "return by the thirteenth" actually meant. Yet in the moment, I was unable to overlook the fact that Feller had just contradicted himself, and I called him on it.

"How is it you claim to not know anything beyond the Fisk at-bat in the twelfth, yet you seem quite confident that the game will make it at least as far as a thirteenth inning?"

As the two of us knew he would, Doyle tapped an easy ground ball out to Concepcion for the second out of the inning. Feller waited until he'd announced Yastrzemski to the plate before drawing some tasty smoke and then embarking on an eye-opening, roundabout route toward his answer.

"For every single version of this game, there are three random representatives who've been flushed back in time from their respective two thousand and sixteens. The same scalper in the Pink Floyd T-shirt is always the ticket distributor, and the same security guard always does her best to keep her guests buried in the past. Your case is unique in that you and Zack happened upon each other. Usually, our visitors presume they're alone and end up meandering into the cold clutches of madness before the first inning is through. You guys basically kept each other … well … *sane.*"

"How do you *know* this shit?" If Feller's mic were on, my words would have carried all the way to Beacon Hill. I'd had enough of him talking to me as if I were a puppet in his play. "How do you know Zack?" I continued with a seething rage I didn't know I had in me. "And how the *fuck* do you know *me*?"

With Yaz quickly down in the count, Feller returned his cigar to the ashtray in an unperturbed manner, as if it might distract him from what he was about to say. "Listen, I don't really *know* anything." His admission of a deeper truth had begun. "This information doesn't come directly from me. I'm more the intermediary voice, so to speak. As the game progresses, I become more informed of the trio's various particulars. In your case, for example, I welcomed you into my booth because I was made aware you were looking to find me."

I wasn't sure that "welcomed" would be the term I'd use to describe how he initially made me feel, but that was neither here nor there. "Made aware by whom?" I asked sharply and then braced for the furthest thing from a run-of-the-mill reply—and, boy, did old Sherm deliver.

"By the yellow button," he stated impassively, as if I should have followed that with *Oh, of course, I should've known.*

Craving some World Series heroics from their slugging left-fielder, the restless Red Sox faithful released a collective sigh as Yastrzemski bounced an easy ground ball to short. The game was headed to the twelfth inning, and according to the handwritten message on the back of my ticket, the ghost of Cruisin' Clarence, and the coarse-grained, smoky words of Feller himself, I had only six outs to play with to get my shit together and find my way back to 2016.

"I'm sorry, but did you say you get your information from the *yellow button*?"

Chuckling at his own words, Feller moved a hand toward the base of his mic but kept his fingers off the buttons. "Forgive me. I'm sure that came across sounding quite ridiculous. What I should've said was that this microphone channels what I can best describe as cosmic feedback. Basically, every time I release this yellow button after making an announcement during this particular game, a piece of information concerning our three arrivals promptly appears in my mind, like a tattooed thought. From that point on, I'm free to use it however I see fit.

"Amid a slew of subordinate details, the feedback told me the means by which you arrived, that you had an encounter with old Clarence, that you're to return by the thirteenth inning, and maybe the most important piece of information where you're concerned, the means by which you're to do it."

I realized, right then and there, that I'd never understand how or truly believe that he was actually receiving "cosmic feedback" through his microphone. Even for someone who'd just plunged forty-one years into the past, the idea of a divine frequency seemed to exceed the boundaries of reason. But all mysteries aside, the fact that he claimed to know how I could find my way home was all I suddenly cared about.

"Well, Mister Feller," I said, rising from the seat in which I was just getting comfortable, "given that the twelfth is upon us, I'd have to say that *now* would be a great time to elaborate on that last little piece of information."

Feller was shaking his head before I'd even finished speaking. I could tell by his eyes that he was genuinely burdened by what he was about to say. "Unfortunately, Landon," he began, "I'm privy to certain things, but I can't always divulge them. The only advice I can offer you is that you gotta get in to get out."

"Advice?" Now Feller was really pushing *my* buttons. "You call that advice? More like another fucking riddle!"

My next move was strictly impulsive. I lunged at Feller and went straight for the microphone's yellow button. He was surprisingly swift, grabbing my forearm and stopping me three inches short of the mark. His grip made it feel like my arm was being compressed in a vice, and as pain shot through my limb, it became clear that he truly believed he was guarding his secrets.

With Feller resisting my arm, I jockeyed around him and pressed the button with my other hand. I released it after a few seconds and then swiped the mic onto the floor along with a rain of paper. Looking back, maybe all of Fenway got a quick, muffled sample of our struggle, but I doubt it penetrated KC and the Sunshine Band's "Get Down Tonight," as the freshly squeezed disco-funk single had the crowd grooving between the late innings. I broke free of Sherm's hold and stomped on his mic, shattering it into an irreparable ruin.

"Are ya privy to *that*?" I barked before heading toward the door.

Feller didn't stop my retreat, but he did call to me before I reached the corridor. "What did it tell you?" he asked composedly, as if our little tussle hadn't winded him in the slightest. "The feedback—what did it tell you?"

I paused, turned slowly to face him, and then lied. "It told me that for the sake of *your* safety, you'd better hope to hell I manage to catch my train back to the future."

A New World Breeze

In truth, the yellow button didn't tell me a damn thing. I was on my own once again, but this time the sands were passing through the hourglass, threatening to bury me in the past.

The twists and turns that led me back to the stairwell were void of any threats. Once I got there, the cook, who'd been snoozing on the couch with a lit cigarette, was sitting hunched on the top step. She'd upgraded her potency of smoke, as the rich, skunky aroma of reefer filled the air.

"There's a game for the ages going on out there," I mentioned as I stood next to her.

She forced a courteous smile. "They could be playing cricket out there for all I care." Then she reached up and offered me a hit, to which I politely declined. "I hope the Sox win though, I could use the money that one last shift would offer."

I wished the woman well and began my descent, which would take me back to the concourse. I made it down maybe four steps before I stopped and turned to face her. Our eyes were on the same plane, her sitting and me standing. It was evident that she could use a break, so I used my knowledge of the future to give her one. I told her to save as much money as possible until the following spring and then place it on the Reds over the Yankees in the '76 World Series. I'd like to think she followed through with my advice and that she lived off her fortuitous riches for some time.

As I neared the base of the stairwell, I heard something that stretched my sanity as thin as it could go without snapping—and I didn't (and still don't) know how the hell it was possible, considering the extensive damage I'd carried out on his mic—the unequivocal voice of Sherm Feller announcing Johnny Bench to the plate to open up the Cincinnati twelfth. His voice was muffled from within the tight quarters of the vertical space, but I swear there was a slight snicker in his delivery that was meant to burrow under my skin. Like a pitcher receiving a sign from his catcher that he wants no part of whatsoever, I shook it off and moved onward.

By the time I'd cleared the STAFF ONLY door and followed the deserted concourse back around to the first-base side of the field, the Reds were already threatening with a pair of runners on and only one out. I had a great view of the action, and as much as I knew I should have been feverishly seeking a way to escape the past, something inside told me to stay put for at least the Concepcion at-bat. Maybe I was playing a hunch, or maybe, just maybe, due to an unfamiliar user, my personal piece of "cosmic feedback" was just coming around after a short technical delay.

On the third pitch, Concepcion sliced a drive down the line in right. "Dewey" Evans broke to his left and scampered to snag it out of the air for the second out of the inning, his momentum carrying him up against the low wall in foul territory. I then spotted what I swore was a familiar figure jogging up the aisle about twenty feet from where Evans steadied himself and returned the ball to the infield. I raced over to meet the man at the top of his climb and was hit with a whirlwind of emotions when I realized he was exactly who I'd thought he was.

It was my buddy, Carlos. The only problem was, he clearly had too much weighing on his mind to recognize me. He was slightly out of breath and continued past me for a few steps before our fellowship registered within him. He stopped in his tracks and slowly turned around as if fearful I might flee if he moved too fast.

The first thing I thought was that I hoped I didn't look as unglued as he did. I'd found him at the right time because he appeared to be on the verge of curling up in the cuckoo's nest.

"Carlos!" I called out, even though he was standing right in front of me. I saw a world of relief wash over him in an instant, and though we were far from a familiar time, seeing a familiar face was a prodigious shot in the arm for both of us.

"How the— How long have—" Initially Carlos couldn't put a sentence together to save his life. I wrapped my arms around him and gave him the tightest hug I've ever given anybody. "To say that I'm happy to see you doesn't even begin to explain it!" he exclaimed with newfound spirit, as if I were squeezing the words out of him. I wanted nothing more than to hear about all he'd been through to that point, but the clock was ticking and the ride home once again required room for two.

I suddenly heard a replay of Feller's words in my mind. *For every single version of this game, there are three random representatives who've been flushed back in time from their respective two thousand and sixteens.* I didn't know exactly how random we were, considering I'd spotted Zack out on Lansdowne before the game, and Carlos and I have known each other for years, but he rounded out our time-travelling triad nonetheless.

There was a grand ovation as Cesar Geronimo was caught looking at strike three to end the top of the twelfth. We both knew who was due to lead off the bottom half of the inning, but only one of us knew that things were about to . . . change.

"Well we can't come this far and not watch Fisk's winner!" Carlos asserted. He was already facing the field, hands clenching the cold steel railing.

I wanted to tell him that we were wasting precious time, that there would be no celebrated home run down the left-field line caroming high off the foul pole and toppling into the glove of a dejected George Foster. The only problem was, as Feller put it, the Fisk at-bat was about to trigger the big fork in the road, and I simply couldn't peel myself away from the prospect of witnessing such a phenomenon.

As Pat Darcy finished warming up on the mound for his third inning of work, Fisk knocked the weighted ring from his weapon and began his slow, contemplative stroll to the plate.

"I need you to brace yourself for something other than what you're expecting right now," I warned, sparing Carlos the details that were too convoluted for the moment.

"What are you goin' on about?" he asked. "In case you didn't know, a timeless piece of baseball history is about to take place, and we're the only ones who know it's comin'."

After alleviating the tightness in his back with a series of twisting stretches, Fisk dug in and watched Darcy's first offering sail high and tight. My heart was pounding in my chest with detrimental force, as I knew the next pitch would be the definition of a game changer.

Carlos whacked me on the upper arm with some authority. "I think this is the pitch!" he declared with a childlike expression that was a far cry from the out-of-sorts mask he was wearing when I'd first found him. It was indeed the second pitch that

Fisk had sent deep into the night, but as far as what was about to happen next, my guess was as good as anyone else's.

Darcy was looking sluggish on the hill, as though part of him wanted to give in and serve up a nice meatball to Fisk just so he could finally hit the showers. I'm certain that he didn't *actually* do it on purpose, but Darcy grooved that next pitch right into Fisk's wheelhouse. The Sox catcher took his patented mighty cut and drove the ball high in an eerily familiar direction. The crowd lifted in a simultaneous roar, and Carlos raised his arms and hollered, "There she goes!"

While everybody in the park was ecstatic with the anticipation of witnessing a game-winning home run, I stood superlatively perplexed. Fisk had smacked a blast that was a carbon copy of the one that, according to Feller, wasn't supposed to be duplicated.

As the ball travelled, I took my eye off it for a second and glanced down at Fisk. He was in the midst of his renowned sideways skip down the first-base line, trying to will his work fair by frantically waving his arms in that direction. Then I zeroed in on the yellow extremity that would be officially named the Fisk Foul Pole in my version of 2005. From our skewed angle, the ball appeared to be heading straight for it, as it towered high above the Green Monster like a golden spire.

In real time, Fisk's drive was probably airborne for no more than three seconds, but as I watched it, it was as if the aging film had been stretched, and the moment played out in slow motion.

The conclusion of the play was unquestionably the most fascinating thing I've ever seen in my life. The ball approached the pole at the same trajectory as the famed home run, but at the last second, it must have caught a new-world breeze and carried ever so slightly to the left, just missing contact by a matter of inches.

To the resentment of thirty-five thousand strong, the moon-shot sailed out of the ballpark and onto Lansdowne Street as no more than a loud strike. The ball had flown foul by the smallest of margins, but the bottom line was that it *did* go foul, and Game 6 of the 1975 World Series continued as a result.

Surprisingly, the first thing that sprung to my mind after the dramatic foul ball was how much I missed the purity of the game. The umpires deemed the ball foul, and that was the end of it. There were no instant replay reviews back then, as the human element was as much a part of the game as Cracker Jacks and high-cut stirrups.

I looked at Carlos and quickly concluded that the purity of the game was the furthest thing from his mind. His face appeared to be frozen in time, as the gears in his head struggled to process the fact that Fisk wasn't jogging around the bases toward a waiting mob of teammates at home plate.

As if convinced that he was simply seeing things, he closed his eyes and gave his head a quick but spirited shake. What he saw when he reopened them was the same thing I was seeing: a hapless Carlton Fisk taking the long walk back to the batter's box, all the while loathing the fact that baseball is, and always will be, a game of inches.

Belly of the Beast

"Okay, what the fuck just happened?" Carlos finally managed to mutter, the look of fear and confusion once again clouding his eyes.

"Welcome to an alternate version of the past, my friend." I spread my arms wide and held them out toward the playing surface. "This is what I tried to warn you about, but you weren't having any of it. Everything that happens in this game from here on out is like some form of ulterior bonus coverage."

Reds manager Sparky Anderson didn't like the fact that Darcy's previous pitch had nearly been deposited in the Charles River, so he shuffled out to the mound to speak with his tiring hurler. Nobody made as many trips to the mound as Anderson, and when he made that particular visit, I couldn't help but be thankful. Carlos and I were down to our final three outs, and Anderson was inadvertently buying us time.

Again, Sherm Feller's voice writhed around in my mind like an undying earworm. *The only advice I can offer you is that you gotta get in to get out.* As cryptic as the advice was, I had no other choice but to try and unravel it. I was almost certain that "out" represented home—as in a safe return to a familiar twenty-first century. It was the "you gotta get in" bit that had me scratching my head. I dreaded that it possibly meant entering the elevator, and I decided I'd settle into a surrogate past before ever setting foot inside that direful ride.

I have to admit I was stumped. It felt as if I were trying to hop on a train home that was steaming through the station at full speed. Though I didn't have a clue where we were headed, I told Carlos we had to move. We had to stir something up, and we had to stir it up fast.

As we advanced along the concourse, I heard the sudden, solid crack of a well-struck ball and immediately knew that Darcy had served up another fat one. Though I'd missed what happened, the crowd was deliriously drunk on the result.

We broke for the nearest opening, and I saw Pudge dusting off his lower half while standing out on second base. I turned to a jubilant gentleman standing to my left and informed him I'd missed the play. "Where did Fisk smack his two-bagger?"

"Ah shit, ya missed it?" the man said in a haze of excitement. He was dressed like a businessman, but looked to be letting it all hang out in the midnight hour. I could tell he was gearing up to give me an elaborate account. "Pudge just belted another one!" He emphasized the drive by pointing out to left field. "More of a liner though, right over Foster's head until it rapped off the scoreboard door on the fly. Foster played the carom horribly, and Fisk took advantage by sneaking into second ahead of the throw."

For some mysterious reason, a piece of his description jumped out at me. "Did you say it went right off the scoreboard door?"

"Yeah, man. If that sucker was open, the Monster would've swallowed it up and spit out the seams right there onto the warning track!"

My stomach did a flip. I was confident I'd found my "you gotta get in." I had to get inside the Green Monster and from within the belly of the beast, hopefully find the means "to get out."

I wanted to hug that godsend of a stranger like I'd hugged Carlos at the top of the aisle, but instead I just advised him to invest in an unpolished little computer software company called Microsoft. He threw me a look that said business hours were closed, but he still jotted the word down on a little notepad he withdrew from his breast pocket. I'd like to think it was the best move he ever made.

I found myself riding a powerful wave of intuition, and as strange as it must have sounded to Carlos when I proposed our next move, he showed a faithful allegiance to the direction of the surge.

I couldn't speak for 1975, but I was certain that for as long as I'd been attending games at Fenway, the only way to gain access behind the Green Monster was through the scoreboard door out in left field. Carlos agreed, but went on to say he vaguely recalled hearing that the scoreboard access hadn't always been the only way in. The specifics didn't come to him right away, as he sought a muddy memory that, theoretically, hadn't even occurred yet.

"Let's think on it as we move," I announced, and we started with a nimble step along the concourse toward the left-field corner.

As if motion started the wheels turning in his mind, Carlos suddenly found the lost information he was after. "Lansdowne Street!" he exclaimed, and I sensed the Gordian knot unravelling in his attic. I knew the back side of the Monster ran along Lansdowne, but I needed more, and he promptly delivered. "It had to've been around the time Papi joined the Sox. I was doing my thing along Lansdowne one afternoon before a game when some old, hunchbacked black fella approached me on the sidewalk and started into a Fenway Park history lesson."

My brain ached with the thought that Carlos was almost certainly referring to a familiar janitorial spectre.

"It was the one and only time I've ever seen him in my life. He was sweeping debris into one of those upright dust-pans when he asked me if I was aware that I was standing directly above the bunker that ran behind the base of the Green Monster. It was news to me at the time—and a neat little quirk in the Fenway architecture—but potential ticket buyers were strolling on by my post, and I attempted to slip his unsought company. Then he raised his dustpan and held it horizontally in front of me like a makeshift boom gate, clearly indicating he wasn't quite through.

"Speaking as if he wasn't hindering my day in the least, he went on to state that, up until the late seventies, an undisclosed hatch-and-ladder access down into the confined quarters rested at the foot of the left-field light tower. It was as if he somehow knew I'd actually need that information one day." Carlos paused, struggling to grasp the shuffled chronology. "That old man's words were more than just an extremely bizarre coincidence, weren't they?"

"I certainly hope so," I replied with an apprehensive taste in my mouth, all the while realizing that Cruisin' Clarence was dusting the frame of a much bigger picture. We were already heading for the stairs that would bring us back down to street level and, thanks to Carlos's timely recollection, closer to a specific light tower along Lansdowne Street.

With Fisk representing the winning run on second base and all eyes peeled on the action, we exited the building like a pair of casual fans who'd seen more than their share of baseball for one night. A comparatively pleasant security guard at the gate offered us a nod and told us to have a safe journey home. I pondered the reality that home was so close and yet so far away. As we departed through the same gate I'd entered some five hours earlier, the archaic turnstile that had spun me into the past was nowhere to be found.

Although the Doobie Brothers wouldn't release the album for another five months, Carlos and I were *Takin' It to the Streets*. Okay, it was more like we made a hard right as soon as we cleared the garage doors and then took about thirty paces along the Lansdowne sidewalk, but props to the Doobies nonetheless. The towering light stanchion hugged the Fenway exterior, and though its bright radiance was aimed out over the field, a soft, mystical glow warmed the street below.

As the entire city of Boston was immersed in the events of the bottom of the twelfth, Lansdowne Street was ours and ours alone. That's the only reason I can think of to explain why nobody had noticed the lonely baseball that had come to rest along the curb, directly across the street from our light tower. It rested inches away from being swallowed by a storm drain. There was, and still is, no doubt in my mind that it was the very ball that Pat Darcy had served up to Fisk when he hooked it foul by a matter of inches. God only knows how many surfaces it ricocheted off before finding its place along the concrete edging.

As I raced over and picked up the ball, my eye was drawn to an unmistakable scuff mark on its surface that only further proved my theory. I buried the inestimable souvenir into my kangaroo pocket and returned to inform Carlos of my find. I began to utter a few words, but he was lost in his own discovery, and considering it involved the task at hand, it took precedence.

"Son of a bitch was right!" Carlos declared while kneeling at the base of the mighty tower. The lower third of the four poles that made up the steel structure were wrapped in a single Fenway-green nylon tarp, and he had already plucked a Swiss Army knife from his pocket and sliced a four-foot vertical gash through the fabric. We ducked through the opening like we were entering the world's tallest tent and found exactly what we were looking for inside.

The tarp that surrounded us was relatively thin and permitted just enough light to seep through for us to distinguish a rustic wooden hatch cover at our feet. Slits of muted light shone between the planks, and a recessed steel handle was free of any form of locking device.

"I think the honour belongs to you, my friend," I said to Carlos, seeing as he was on a roll, and he was the one who'd been made aware of the hatch in the first place.

A pair of rusty hinges begged for oil as Carlos pulled the cover upward with minimal effort. Somebody had jokingly spray-painted EMERGENCY EGG SHIT on the underside. A thick, musty smell rose up through the mouth like the breath of a sick animal. An eight-rung steel ladder was mounted to a cold concrete wall and led down into the cavernous stretch.

Peering into the access, the light was ominously pale, and neither of us was particularly eager to hop on in. *You gotta get in to get out.* Like the one Clarence had mumbled as he swept his nook, the phrase was becoming a goddamn mantra. Knowing we were doomed if we weren't on the right track, I hit the ladder first and instructed Carlos to leave the lid open behind us.

Expecting to touch down on the concrete landing, an unforeseen lump threw off my balance, and an accompanying ear-piercing squeak announced our arrival. A brown rat the size of a squirrel scurried to a safe distance and then turned to hiss at me before continuing his retreat. I'd heard countless tales about the rats that roamed Fenway's depths, but I certainly wasn't expecting my first step to be a personal introduction to it.

Carlos joined me down below, and in a hushed voice I warned him of our furry company. We were in a cramped space no bigger than a small shed, and it seemed to be strictly for discarded materials. A bulky concrete partition yielded a minimal one-foot passage to the main stretch behind the Green Monster.

I peered through the opening and saw a sizeable NBC television camera resting on a stand about fifteen feet away. The cameraman was aiming its eye at the action on the field through a designated slot in the wall. His ears were covered by a headset, and his focus was fixed on the picture he was producing . . . until the portly rodent I'd nearly turned into a pancake took to something tasty on the top of his shoe. The cameraman jerked and turned with the disturbance, and I ducked back behind the partition. After giving him a moment to return his attention to the game, we made our move.

I led the way into the depths of the narrow space, sneaking behind the engrossed cameraman. When I looked back to see if he'd detected us, his face remained buried within the shield of the ridiculously large viewfinder. I spotted the rat scampering back to the room we'd started from, its tail slithering behind like a garter snake stapled to its ass.

It felt as if we'd set foot inside a dank, lengthy catacomb. The only thing around us that wasn't solid concrete was the reverse side of the scoreboard where the number slots resembled vaults that housed the dead. Bulbs in wire cages lined the low cap and gave off a wash of feeble light. White and yellow numbers on green metal plates hung from rebar spikes that jutted from the signature-covered back wall, and rectangular eye-level openings the size of mail slots enabled a view of the field through the Monster.

The scoreboard door that Fisk had punished with his screaming line drive was now right in front of us, and I wondered if he was still stuck on second base. As if to test our place within our strange new world, Carlos took out his pocket knife and etched a *16* into the door's surface, and then dusted the green filings from the scribe.

Now that we were actually roiling in the belly of the beast, we still didn't have a clue as to what we were after. We moved along the back of the wall but continued to find ourselves at a loss. I'd expected to have noticed the scoreboard operator doing his thing by that point, but apart from the cameraman, the entire span was vacant of personnel. Another cluster of metal plates dangled from rebar along the back wall. They were rectangular and featured abbreviated team names. A small table along the concrete wall between a pair of chairs was hosting a game of chess that, at least for the moment, had been abandoned. Next to the board, an ashtray contained a heaping pile of cigarette butts, and I was certain that the next one to be placed on top would bring the entire mountain down in an avalanche of residual filth.

When I heard Feller announce Dwight Evans to the plate, I promptly found one of the small slots in the wall and assessed how the inning was unfolding. I noticed that Fisk had found his way to third at some point, and with Evans coming up with nobody else aboard, I figured there already had to be two down.

Carlos was peering through the slot next to mine, and he was the first to notice Sparky Anderson bounce out of the dugout to finally remove Darcy. The legendary Reds manager had gone by many names, but his penchant for drying up his bullpen on a near-nightly basis had earned him the moniker "Captain Hook," and he was at it once again in the twelfth. To be honest, I was surprised that Sparky had another arm at his disposal, and when Clay Kirby came loping in from the pen, I knew he was burning his last resort.

I don't think Kirby had even reached the infield dirt when an enraged voice barked at us from the far end of the subterraneous wing. "Hey! Yah not allowed back eah!" The Bostonian accent was so thick within the confined space that it felt like I could scrape it off the walls.

We jumped from our view of the field and turned to our left to measure the source.

"This is a fahkin' restricted ahrea!"

A man appeared to have come through a similar one-foot opening on his own end, and he cursed our presence as he marched toward us. A second man poured through the same gap and raced to his partner's side when he heard the commotion.

I imagined how the unvarnished truth would sound. *Well, hello there, fine scoreboard operators of a bygone era. Me and my friend here have recently travelled back in time from two thousand sixteen. So, if you'll excuse us, we'd just like to snoop around a little, as we've been led to believe that somewhere back here lies a portal that we need to find before one more out is recorded on the field.*

Both men were much bigger (and uglier) than Carlos and me. I pictured their employer saying, "We're glad to have the pair of you on board here at Fenway, but we're going to stick you underground and behind this massive green wall where no one will ever have the displeasure of seeing your homely faces."

Considering the abuse my body had endured since I'd arrived, I wanted no part of a physical confrontation. I was just about to offer a peaceful introduction when Carlos suddenly made it clear he was ready to deal from a drastically different angle.

"What are you clowns hiding in that room back there?" he challenged our new company.

I shot him a disapproving gaze, hoping he'd realize I wasn't on board with his approach, all the while bracing myself for the unwanted shitstorm I figured was about to rain down on us.

The man who'd been doing the talking was ready to throw down. He was a brutish figure who had rage searing in his deep-set eyes—eyes that had yet to blink. He spun his Sox cap backwards on his dome and then stained the ground beside him with a spray of gritty tobacco juice. Carlos was lining up to dance with the lout, when the other man intervened with a double stiff arm.

"Whoa, whoa, whoa, fellas," he began in a measured tone. His voice was guttural and grating, similar to that of Feller's. He looked to be a little older than his partner, and I could tell he was the one calling the shots behind the Monster. "Let's dial it down a nahtch a two, shall we?" the accent was there, but not nearly as evident. "We can't be down eah tradin' blows with Louie down tha hall tryin' to concentrate on the action." He nodded toward the cameraman. Carlos and the brute relaxed their shoulders and exhaled some of their tension.

"How'd yuz know 'bout tha hatch?" the brute asked. He'd simmered down some, but I was almost certain that the wrong answer would bring him back to a boil. "There ain't moah than a half dozen people even know it exists!"

Though Carlos had been the one to receive the information about the hatch, he'd turned to stone on me and inadvertently backed me into a corner—a corner where hesitation would be our undoing. So, I gave the men a reply I could neither confirm nor deny. "We learned of its whereabouts from Cruisin' Clarence."

Now I had *three* faces staring at me, each in their own bemused manner. The scoreboard operators looked at me in a way that suggested they knew the name but struggled to believe the deceased janitor knew any more about Fenway than where to dump his dustpan. Carlos furrowed his brow, clearly unaware that a little acquiescence would have gone a long way.

"Cruisin' Clarence?" The man in charge repeated the name in a tone that implied he would have been less surprised if I'd said "Babe Ruth."

I had to sell it, and I had to sell it fast. "Last year, before he left us, of course, old Clarence blew a tire and took a nasty spill out on Lansdowne as he was about to enter the park. I was only about twenty feet behind him, and I witnessed him go down. Poor old guy hurt his hip somethin' severe that day. I notified security to call for an ambulance, and then I waited by his side until it arrived." I could tell by their body language that their patience was wearing about as thin as my bullshit story. "While we waited, he became delirious with pain, and just before he blacked out, for whatever reason, he pointed to the base of the light tower and made me aware of the covert access."

"There's no way that bottom-feeding janitah knew 'bout the bloody hatch!" the brute protested sharply. "And even if 'e did, and 'e actually puked up that information intah ya lap, then why'dja wait so long to explore this space? Or have yuz already been down eah before?"

Carlos and I locked eyes and realized we were spinning our wheels on a muddy road that would inevitably leave us mired in the past. We needed traction, and our little game of question-and-answer wasn't getting us anywhere.

The two men circled in front of us, fortuitously affording us an opening in the direction from which they had come. Like a green beacon blinking at us from the future, we simultaneously saw that lane as a dragstrip home. Then, like the classic zeitgeist album that would, curiously enough, be unleashed on America exactly two years from that very day, we made for it like a *Bat Out of Hell*.

A Christian in the Devil's Cage

Carlos and I were a good dozen steps into our dash when I realized we weren't even being pursued. The men who had accosted us knew the layout of their underground lair and understood we had no escape route where we were heading.

Marginally winded, we reached a concrete wall so pitted and worn it resembled the surface of the moon. There was still the modest opening from which the two men had leaked, but I was certain the space beyond it would mirror the one we'd descended into from the ladder—minus a ladder, of course.

With nowhere else to go but onward, I shuffled sideways through the opening. I wondered how the brute, who surely had a good eighty pounds on me, managed to suck his gut in far enough to fit. Carlos was a slender stretch, as all he had to do was tuck his shoulders and step through squarely. He glanced back at the men before joining me in the back room; each was wielding a four-foot rebar rod.

The back room was exactly what I presumed it would be: the end of the line. There were no more gaps to squeeze through or ladders leading back up to the street. The only outlets permitting escape were flush with the ground, no more than the size of a quarter and strictly limited to critters.

The room was nothing more than a bookend space of miscellaneous clutter. A kerosene lamp rested on a small wooden table tucked into a corner; it filled the space with a warm amber glow. An enormous electrical panel occupied most of one wall, with conduits feeding into the power source from every possible direction. A slipshod stash of metal plates with faded numbers filled another corner, and a sturdy wooden workbench sat smack-dab in the middle like a rectangular island. *You gotta get in to get out.* By that point, I wanted to yank a loose thread from that cursed phrase and watch the whole thing unravel into the burning pit of hell. All it had done was lead me down the wrong road and straight to a terminus of space and time.

We could hear the men advancing, their brash voices announcing their approach. As much as we wanted nothing to do with a hostile encounter—especially involving weapons—we still needed something to defend ourselves against the potential swings and jabs of cold rebar. Carlos circled the workbench and discovered a mighty crowbar resting against a leg; I found . . . well, let's just say I found something that must have left those bruisers thinking we'd escaped through the bloody rat holes.

I'd noticed a moth-eaten burlap blanket spread over a mishmash of jutting shapes. A particular object underneath it had toppled over at some point, and a good portion of it was exposed in the lamplight. It was a brass stanchion eerily similar to the ones I'd sent tumbling over in the moments before the present gave way to the past.

I lifted a corner of the burlap and noticed the other stanchions still standing upright. With my heart thumping, I gripped the coarse fabric with both hands and peeled the rest of it clean off the pile of assorted goods . . . and there it was! Its tapered column stood like a pillar of stability, and its tetrad of arms secured the collage of clutter in place. There, in all its transcendental glory, was the archaic turnstile.

As I stumbled upon my auspicious discovery, the two men arrived at our door, and they weren't selling cookies.

"Stall 'em!" I hissed at Carlos. "I just need a minute or two . . . Go!"

I practically shoved the poor guy through the opening and then hustled back to wreak havoc on the orderly arrangement. With no regard for how or where the items came to rest, I tossed aside aeration tools, corrugated field signs, paint cans, folded chairs, and a weighty tamper that nearly cost me my lower back. When the stanchions inevitably got a taste of my sudden destructive streak, they clanked together in a familiar toll and then succumbed to gravity like chopped trees in a forest.

After kicking aside a few smaller objects around its base, I grabbed one of the turnstile's arms and schlepped that sturdy bastard forward five feet into the open. By that point, Carlos had already left the room and been promptly bulldozed right back again. But he miraculously managed to straddle the crowbar across the one-foot opening to hinder their passage. They jabbed at him with their rebar and kicked savagely at his shins (a pain I knew all too well), but he held his ground and afforded me time to do what had to be done.

Impulsiveness nearly had me propelling myself through the turnstile's rotating arms but I was stalled by the thought of poor Carlos, who was taking more than enough lumps for the two of us. I certainly couldn't recount these events if I'd chosen to abandon him when the going got tough, leaving him outnumbered in the depths of time.

Not once did I consider that the turnstile might not be the same one, that maybe it was a similar relic that just happened to be stashed back there. Nor did I wonder if it would allow me to bring a companion through the rotating pivot and along for the ride.

Suddenly, I recalled the World Series ticket I'd received from the mysterious scalper and wondered if I'd be able to return home without it. That was when I made the timely connection between Carlos and his scalped tickets—could he have possibly retained some unsold tickets for the game I'd intended to catch?

"Tell me you've still got some tickets on ya!" I said desperately as I sprang to his side.

Sweat was dripping profusely from his brow, diluting blood from a slender gash across his cheek. "Tickets?" He seemed to wrestle the word from his lips as he continued to stonewall the scoreboard operators with his crowbar. He'd already bought me the time I needed to haul the turnstile out to where it could spin without restriction, but now I needed him to focus on what I had to say.

"Listen to me! We're gonna have to make a run at this!"

"Make a run at what?" He demanded in the midst of his struggle. I was pressing my weight against both Carlos and his crowbar, trying to spare him some of the intruding barbarity.

"This'll sound absurd, but you have to trust what I'm about to say. And then you have to act on it no matter how foolish it may seem."

Carlos nodded his affirmation as he struggled. I felt the force of the men bearing down on us and marvelled at how Carlos and his slim frame had managed to fend them off for so long.

"On the other side of the workbench is an old turnstile," I said, speaking in short puffs of breath, "and when I say *now,* we're gonna break for it and then push on through—just like we would if we were entering a ballpark. But first I need you to dig out a pair of tickets—from the game in sixteen. Hand me one of 'em and hold on tight to the other one!"

As my arms and legs trembled with exertion, I sensed it wouldn't be long before they'd overpowered us and started swinging their rebar at our heads like they were high fastballs. Carlos released his hold on the crowbar with one hand and dipped into an inside pocket. After fishing around for what seemed like an eternity, he withdrew the coveted prizes and handed me what I hoped would be my permit back to a familiar place in time.

The moment I seized the ticket, the dam broke, and the men surged forward like an angry torrent. They forced the crowbar to the ground, and it rattled to a halt at the foot of the ingress.

"NOW!" I yelled. With the ticket locked in my sweaty grasp and the memories of the adventure stowed in the overhead compartment of my mind, I broke for the turnstile, praying we'd come out on the other side of forty-one years.

I met one of the revolving arms and gave it a good nudge, but it was decidedly arthritic, as if the weight of four decades was resisting the device's mobility. Then Carlos applied force to the arm behind me, and it felt as if the pivot had received a timely shot of oil. I felt the same slight shock that had zapped me during my first go-round. The sights and sounds around me dimmed and waned into an ebonized silence, and I smelled the distinct odour of sulphur.

I wish I could better define the chimerical void that is time travel. Wherever or *when*ever I was, I was conscious of the moment. I wasn't exactly propelled into the future, but rather I remained stationed in the void, and the future came to *me*, floating down gracefully from above like a celestial mist.

The next thing I recall was hearing the low rumble of rolling thunder as it vibrated in my chest. I felt groggy, like the deep resonance had just shaken me from sleep, but I was on my feet and Carlos was standing next to me.

The smallest amount of warm light kindled our surroundings, but it was enough to discern we were still in the back room nestled below Lansdowne Street and hidden behind the most famous wall in baseball history. It was the same room, but I was certain we'd spanned four decades to get there.

The space was far less cluttered, and it was, thankfully, free of the stale, reeky air that permeated the past. I half expected to find an old programs booth tucked away in a forgotten corner. There was no booth, but though worse for wear, the workbench still served as the room's centrepiece. The turnstile was nowhere to be found.

The skies over present-day Boston continued to grumble like an empty stomach, and the thrumming sound of heavy rain had begun to accompany it. Carlos and I had yet to utter a single word when a foreign voice shattered the silence, calling out from what seemed to be the far end of the underground channel.

"Come on out, boys," the speaker instructed in a composed, yet stern manner. He sounded middle-aged, tired, and somewhat testy. "It's been a long day for all of us."

Carlos and I grinned uneasily at each other. "Is it possible that somebody's expecting us?" Carlos asked in a hushed tone.

I tried to come up with some clever way of stating that logically it would be an impossibility, but given the number of impossibilities we'd just refuted in the flesh, *logic* was still limping around in my mind with a bad knee and a bruised shin. "There's only one way to find out," I said finally, and we walked toward the voice.

An initial glance failed to reveal anyone along the narrow stretch, so we proceeded with caution.

Things hadn't changed much within the belly of the beast. The lighting was as feeble as ever. Numbered plates still hung from rebar spikes, and the odd table and chair still had a home along the back wall. A refrigerator was a nice touch, and other than about ten thousand fresh signatures scattered about the cold concrete, the appliance looked to be about the only addition made in the last four decades by the underground design team. A few lines from classic Tom Petty songs were stencilled on the walls in blue and red paint, and I recalled reading a piece about Christian Elias, Fenway's current scoreboard operator, and why he chose the particular words of his favourite rock 'n' roll artist.

"Hello?" Carlos offered reluctantly into the void. The word bounced off the walls like a rubber ball in a squash court.

Another dozen steps took us past a protruding column, and that was when I first spotted Mister Elias himself sitting comfortably at a small desk facing the back wall, feverishly hacking away at the keys of a laptop computer, his eyes attentively fixed on the screen.

"Come pull up next to me, fellas," he uttered from a hole in his concentration. A pair of chairs were already arranged to accommodate us, and we seated ourselves in his questionable company.

Christian stopped typing, took a deep breath, and joggled his head as if shaking away sleep. The chill in the air didn't seem to faze him, as he sat comfortably in the thinnest of jackets. A blue-and-green Hartford Whalers mesh cap was pulled down snug on his head, and his brown hair curled out from underneath it. A thick beard covered his face; it was well-suited to the early fall season.

Elias was in the twilight of his career behind the wall, a job that had been offered to him out of pity when he couldn't crack the grounds crew. At the time, he'd wrinkled his nose and said he'd muster through for one summer. Little did he know that he'd fall in love with the job and eventually work more than nineteen hundred games over a twenty-six-year span.

He powered up a printer stationed next to his laptop, and it beeped and flashed to life. As a document printed (what I assumed he'd been working on), he turned slowly to face us, studying our eyes.

"Christian Elias," he said, introducing himself, "and you have my permission to tell anybody you want about your time-travelling experience. You can also use my real name and explain my role in the grand design.

"They'll never believe you," he continued with a laugh. "And if I'm ever questioned, I'll brush you off as a couple of crazies who I've never seen before in my entire life."

I already knew I'd be writing down my adventure as soon as I had the chance (how could I not?). But after transcribing the events, I can't really say I'd blame readers if they fluffed it off as fiction. On the other hand, if even a single soul believes what I'm saying to be true, then my sharing this with the world will be entirely worth the effort.

Christian knew everything. And when I say *everything*, I mean *ev-'ry-thing*. As you can imagine, Carlos and I had present-day questions that were rooted in the past, but we barely drew them to the surface—we didn't have to. Christian told us to sit back and relax, and then he caught us up to speed by divulging the essential details of our journey.

He assured us that we'd returned to the same day and that it existed within the same world. We'd lost the roughly five hours we spent in 1975, as they'd passed in the present just the same.

The game I'd intended to catch had survived a minimal delay, as the rains had come earlier than expected. In the end, the Sox had prevailed over the Reds by an eerily familiar score of 7–6.

From there, Elias worked backwards into the past. He focused initially on Carlos, and I quickly learned he'd endured a great deal more than I knew before we met up on the concourse. Then he shifted to me and recalled my spellbinding stint in the company of the legendary Sherm Feller.

"The yellow button." He stirred the memory of Feller's old mic to the surface of the present. "The one that he said feeds him information through 'cosmic feedback,' well . . . that feedback is basically *me* communicating with him across the void of time through a traversable electromagnetic wormhole." Christian paused, seeing in my befuddled expression that he was losing me; he tried to dumb it down a little. "Ever see the movie *Frequency*?"

"Sure. The sci-fi flick with Dennis Quaid." I replied, building up the nerve to talk to him. "But that's the movies, man. That kinda shit doesn't *actually happen.*"

"Betcha woulda said the same about time travel before today." He had me on that one. "And how was it possible that Feller kept living through the same game over and over again— but only until the Fisk at-bat in the twelfth, when a common world apparently split into a myriad of different avenues?"

Elias took a few seconds to absorb my query. "I'll offer you this," he said with a cunning eye. "Picture Feller as something akin to a central station anchored in time. When people set out from his post, their view is always limited to their own track, when in truth, there is an innumerable number of tracks all around them, and they all link up with an innumerable number of stations up the line. I could go on, as there is so much more to Feller's otherworldly being, but the secrets behind certain designs are forever locked away in the creator's mind, with the key stowed safely in his warm belly."

Christian reached over to the printer and gathered the documents that were resting in the tray, hot off the press. I wondered what the hell he was working on, and why he was doing it in our presence.

At that point, something caught Carlos's attention on the reverse side of the scoreboard door, which was less than ten feet away from Christian's desk. Carlos popped out of his seat, and as he drew closer, he shouted, "It's gone!" He put his hand on the spot on the door where he'd etched the number sixteen and it all came rushing back to me. "The sixteen!" he said emphatically, "It must've faded over time!"

Christian slid open a drawer next to him and casually withdrew a pair of manila folders along with two white envelopes, all the while reminding Carlos that "time" had nothing to do with it. "Your engraving didn't fade, my friend, or get covered with a layer or two of paint, for that matter. You have to remember that when you actually did it, you were sojourning in another world, which explains why it isn't here today—it was *never* here."

Suddenly, I was reminded of the treasure I'd stashed in the front pouch of my hoodie. I fumbled through the pocket for the ball I'd found along the gutter of an alternate Lansdowne Street.

When my search came up empty, Christian shook his head ever so slightly, and I knew my souvenir was history (pun intended).

Christian placed three pieces of paper and an envelope into each of the folders. Then he tucked the folders under his arm and rose to his feet. "Let's get outta here," he said spiritedly. "Sounds like the rain may've let up for the moment."

I followed him to the door, where he paused and handed Carlos and me each a folder, assertively stating we weren't to so much as thumb through them before we'd exited the ballpark entirely. He grabbed the door's inner handle and flicked a switch next to it that left the entire stretch behind us in a cold sea of darkness. "After yous," he said as he swung the scoreboard door open, and then allowed us to step through.

The fresh air was a kiss of life, as the finest of mists drizzled down over the outfield grass. It felt as if I'd literally been cooped up behind the Monster for forty-one years, like an imprisoned Yankee fan. The lights still illuminated the deserted shrine from high above, and a white tarp blanketed the entire infield like a colossal postage stamp, protecting the basepaths and pitcher's mound from the elements.

Christian clicked the door shut behind us, the sound a soft reverberation within the silent bowl that was our surroundings. I turned and was shocked to find that the son of a bitch had abandoned us by sneaking back into his cave. Carlos and I stood alone with the night, out on the moistened warning track.

Needless to say, the access was unbreachable, but that didn't keep us from rapping against it as if it were the devil's rusty cage. We knew there wasn't a chance in hell that Elias would respond, so, after a short time, we simply took our folders and made for the exit.

We crossed the sacred patch of grass that has been patrolled by such greats as Williams, Yastrzemski, and Ramirez, to name a few, and then we hopped a short wall behind third base before climbing an aisle to the main concourse. A spring-loaded door leading out to Brookline Avenue had our names on it, and we cabbed it back to my apartment to study the contents of Christian's parting gifts.

As I write, it's been eight days since the events that fill these pages. During that stretch, I've spent an unhealthy number of hours on this piece, trying to incorporate as many details as I can possibly draw from the pores of my memory. And I'd like to reiterate here that everything I've included is as true as a Red Sox fan's passion for their team.

As for the folders that Carlos and I received from Christian before he deserted us, two of the three pages within were a summary of the world we'd entered the instant Fisk's deep drive sailed to the left of the foul pole. From that precise moment on, like we've all seen and read in the works of science fiction, the butterfly effect essentially forged a new future.

Not a soul (other than Carlos and me, of course) left the park for at least another hour that night, as the Sox went on to win the game in the bottom of the fourteenth, courtesy of a throwing error by Concepcion that allowed a hustling Doyle to score from second on a routine grounder to short. The Sox also went on to win the World Series the following night with a convincing 10–2 drubbing in Game 7—imagine that! The Curse of the *Who*?

I find it absolutely fascinating how much the entire world changed simply because a baseball missed a pole by a matter of inches. I'll spare you the details of how things completely spun out of control by the late 1980s; that's not what *my* story is about. All I'll say is that if you were to peer through a window that offered a glimpse of *that* 2016, the scene would make the setting of Cormac McCarthy's *The Road* seem like a sunny day in San Diego. Trust me, when put into a parallel-world perspective, things are just peachy in the world we know. Maybe "appreciation" is the underlying theme here.

As I mentioned, Christian also left us each an envelope. It felt practically weightless, and the flap wasn't sealed, making it readily accessible.

I slipped it open and fished out a pair of baseball tickets. *The* tickets, their dates nearly forty-one years apart—October 1975 and September 2016—like chronological bookends. Other than different seat numbers, Carlos's envelope contained the same two tickets, and though they take the cake as far as keepsakes go, we couldn't help but wonder if there was a particular motive behind Christian gifting them to us.

This brings me to the third and final page within the folder. It was headed CONCERNING THE TICKETS. The delivery that followed was typed in a sizeable font, as if to emphasize its weight.

TIME IS AN ILLUSION: ADMIT ONE

Keep the wheel turning

Seat 'em high up along the left-field line

Bring 'em home by the thirteenth

Keep the wheel turning

TIME IS AN ILLUSION: ADMIT ONE

After racking my brain trying to construe its message, I've ultimately chosen to believe that the cryptic bulletin is a licence of sorts—a documented endorsement to share my story, to open the scoreboard door wide and invite the reader inside the belly of the beast. ADMIT ONE.

Now that the tale has been told, I plan to put it aside for a while to allow both it, and myself, to breathe. The work has been consuming my days and nights like a vampire draining my exposed neck, and I'm in need of some serious replenishment.

Before I know it, the winter season will sneak up and cast its fleecy shroud over New England and beyond. So, in the coming days, I'll be heading west on a lengthy road trip to an inner suburb of Cincinnati called Blue Ash. When I arrive, I plan to seek out someone who, in a short time, I came to know only as Zack, to see if his enigmatic elevator not only let him off on the right floor along the vertical chute of time, but also within the contours of the right world.

Extra Innings
Back from Blue Ash

Not only did I *find* Zack McEwan in Blue Ash, I brought him back to Boston to catch a playoff game. Oddly enough, the expedition was his brainchild, and we circled October 10th on the calendar. While still in Ohio, I contacted Carlos, and he secured premium seats behind the plate for the three of us.

Cleveland was in town, and they were already leading the best-of-five series two games to none. In what turned out to be David Ortiz's swan song, the Sox fell 4–3 and were swept away by an Indians squad that caught fire at the right time. Though the result was disappointing, our spirits remained charged, as our gathering was more a celebration of our magical experience in 1975.

Carlos and Zack never (knowingly) crossed paths during our time in the past, but when we convened as a trio to reminisce, it was as if we'd been together in spirit the entire time, tackling our tribulations as a steadfast unit.

On our way back to Boston, I made Zack aware of Christian Elias and his transcendent hand in the entire ordeal. When Elias's name surfaced during the game, Carlos informed us that he'd read it was officially his final season as Fenway's manual scoreboard operator. So, in retrospect, I guess Big Papi stole his spotlight, as far as finales go.

From a distance, we watched the numbered plates being swapped in and out from behind the Green Monster, and on one occasion during the home-half of the eighth, Carlos swore he spotted a pair of steely eyes peering directly at us through one of the small slots in the wall.

I promised Zack I'd drive him all the way back to Ohio the following day, which I did, but our love of the game steered us on a detour up into Cleveland, where we caught Game 1 of the ALCS between the Indians and the Toronto Blue Jays. Cleveland and Bauer's bloody finger steamrolled through that series in five games to advance to the World Series.

On the night of November 2nd, the Chicago Cubs out-lasted "The Tribe" in what many call the greatest Game 7 in World Series history. But the thing is, to me, the Cubbies actually winning it all still seems a little . . . *off*, doesn't it? Kind of makes me wonder if my train still isn't quite rolling along on the proper track—a track where the Curse of the Billy Goat should still be hovering over Wrigley Field like a black cloud, and Ortiz should decide that one more season in Boston would be the perfect ending to a fairy-tale career.

About the Author

Steve Godsoe has always been a huge fan of baseball and science fiction tales. Writing The Turnstile gave him the opportunity to weave his two passions together. Steve, along with his wife, Lindsay, is halfway to his goal of attending a game in every Major League city. The author lives in Stoney Creek, Ontario.

Printed in Canada